The
Boy
with the
Eggshell
skull

The Boy with the Eggshell Skull

Brandon Robshaw

SCHOLASTIC
PRESS

Scholastic Children's Books,
Commonwealth House, 1–19 New Oxford Street,
London WC1A 1NU, UK
a division of Scholastic Ltd
London ~ New York ~ Toronto ~ Sydney ~ Auckland

First published by Scholastic Ltd, 1997

Copyright © Brandon Robshaw, 1997

ISBN 0 590 54235 4

Typeset by DP Photosetting, Aylesbury, Bucks
Printed by Cox & Wyman Ltd, Reading, Berks

10 9 8 7 6 5 4 3 2 1

Chapter One
The Three Conspirators

The scene resembled nothing so much as a conspirators' den, which is not surprising since that is exactly what it was. Fungi sprouted between the damp stone slabs of the walls; somewhere out of sight, rats could be heard scuttering about. The only light came from a clutch of candles stuck in bottles on a rickety wooden table, for though the house could boast electricity, the wiring did not extend to the cellar. Other bottles, containing beer, also stood on the table and whenever one of them was emptied, one of the conspirators would stick a candle in it to shed a little more light on the situation, and crack open a fresh bottle.

The conspirators were three in number. The

largest of them was a huge, lumpy, bald man with thick features reminiscent of a toad – a mournful toad that had experienced a lot of troubles in life. He wore a heavy roll-neck sweater which came right up to his chin and had damp patches at the armpits. A strong whiff of perspiration arose from him whenever he shifted in his seat.

Though the most physically commanding of the three he seemed to defer to the conspirator sitting opposite, who was in every respect his physical antithesis – being, in the first place, a woman. She was thin and gaunt and had dead straight, dead black hair which fell to her waist. She wore an ill-fitting cotton dress and shivered from time to time as if cold. Even in the dimness her face seemed unnaturally pale, except for the dark, deep-set caverns that were her eyes. She, in her turn, seemed to defer to the third conspirator, never interrupting him or venturing to press a contradiction.

He was usually referred to as "the Crow" and looking at him it was easy to see why. He sat with hunched shoulders in the posture of a carrion bird; his nose was so long and ended so sharply you really feared he might give you a nasty peck with it if annoyed. A thatch of spiky black hair decorated his rounded head. He smoked a cheroot from which the smoke curled upwards like ectoplasm at a seance, in grotesque patterns and spirals, in fleeting glimpses of monsters and demons and leering faces.

"Barney Spofforth is the boy's name," said the Crow, "and he's ideal. He might have been manufactured to our specifications."

"The dad's rich, is he?" asked the bald man. "I mean, really rich."

"He's as rich as Midas. As rich as Croesus." The Crow liked to spice his talk with classical allusions and was delighted when people did not understand them. He was widely read in translations of Greek and Latin literature and was fond of telling people he had been to Oxford. When they asked which college, he would answer variously Balliol, Christ Church, Wadham, St John's et cetera as the fancy took him; and each answer was true, for he had visited them all on day-trips. He liked to think he could have been the Master of an Oxford college, had he not become a Master Criminal, as he liked to call it, instead.

"Even you, Edgar," he went on, "must have a

dim recollection somewhere in that concrete brain of yours of Spofforth's Soups. Only the finest hand-picked ingredients, fresh from the country, lovingly prepared in a factory outside Slough. Gamekeeper's broth. Barley and venison. Cream of leek with a hint of dill. Smoked trout velouté. Cornish crab and cream. And this is to say nothing of his mustard or his gravy granules. The man controls one per cent of supermarket shelf space in Great Britain alone. And this is to say nothing of the international market. You can even buy his soups in France – and our Gallic friends think themselves very discerning on the subject of soup."

"My brain's not made of concrete," Edgar protested. "It's made of the same stuff yours is."

"There's just less of it, that's all," the woman told him.

"Thank you, Stella, for those apt words. To continue: the best thing about our Mr Spofforth is that he doesn't spend his money. No yachts. No Porsches. No swimming-pools. He's only interested in his collection."

"What does he collect?"

"Money."

"If he's such a miser," said his wife, "it might not be so easy to get him to cough up."

"Oh, but I think he will cough up. I think he will expectorate three million pounds sterling into our laps without delay. The boy's peculiar infirmity gives us just the leverage we require. He daren't take any risks where such a fragile child is concerned. Leverage, you see. Archimedes said that if you gave him a place to stand he could move the Earth. We have a place to stand and we shall be able to move Mr Spofforth's dusty old wallet. A clever fellow, Archimedes. Have you heard of him, Edgar? A Greek mathematician."

"I don't know no Greeks," Edgar replied. "But I think this could be a bit dodgy, with the kid being infirmary. What if he dies on us? We'll look well sick then. Victor wouldn't have had nothing to do with it."

There was a silence. Then the Crow said: "If you have anything to say about Victor Jabès, it had better not be uttered in my presence. I don't wish to hear the name mentioned again. Do you understand?"

"If you think Jabès is such a wonder-man, why

don't you go and work for him?" enquired Stella nastily. "We can do without you."

But the Crow countermanded this suggestion. "You don't go near Victor Jabès," he said. "Do you understand? Take one step in his direction and I'll cut your legs off."

Edgar understood.

"You've got the easy part, anyway," Stella told him. "All you've got to do is drive the car and then stand guard over the kid when we've got him."

Edgar shrugged philosophically, causing an odour of sweat to rise into the air and hover around him. "Suppose we might as well get going then," he said.

"I'll tell you when to get going," the Crow told him sharply. He placed a bag on the table. "Here's your police uniform, Stella. But don't put it on until you get to England. The kid starts school tomorrow so pick him up the day after. You won't have any trouble. Kids will trust a woman every time. All right, now you can get going. What's that noise?"

"What noise?"

The Crow wheeled round in his chair and stared up at the top of the stairs. The door had swung ajar and around it peeped a small, white, oval face.

"Lucretia! What are you doing out of bed?"

"I couldn't sleep."

She advanced into the room. It could now be seen that her face was not just white, but dead white, almost blindingly white, like a piece of paper with a spotlight trained on it. Even her mother's face, by comparison, seemed to take on a healthy tinge. She looked rather like Wednesday out of the Addams Family, but older, taller and with a more humorous, inquisitive expression.

"Where's Mum going?"

"Have you been eavesdropping?" the Crow demanded. "What did you hear?"

"Nothing – I just heard you say it was time to go –"

"Your mother's going on a business trip for a couple of days. And it's her business, not yours, so keep your nose out of it, understand? And now you're going back to bed. I'll read you a story. A bit of Greek tragedy's what you need."

"Oh no, not nasty old Greek tragedy!"

"Yes," said the Crow sternly. "Some Sophocles. Don't argue. A spot of *Oedipus at Colonus* will do you good."

When they had gone, Edgar opened another bottle of beer and said: "If you want my opinion, it's asking for trouble to bring a kid on a thing like this."

"Nobody wants your opinion."

"There must have been someone you could leave her with –"

"Shut it!" said Stella fiercely. "Our daughter's not a piece of left luggage. Where we go, she goes. She's not well, she needs a lot of looking after in her condition. When you have kids of your own – which will probably be never – maybe you'll understand."

"I just meant, if the kid blabs –"

"She won't blab! She won't know a thing about it. And who could we leave her with anyway? What would we say? 'Could you kindly look after Lucretia for a few weeks while we go off and do a bit of kidnapping?'"

"What about that French woman who owns this house? Your sister-in-law. Annie or whatever she's called."

"Annick? Are you joking? Or are you insane? She's my *ex*-sister-in-law, anyway; I haven't seen her since Geoff died and she hasn't seen Lucretia for years. I never even liked her; I wouldn't have got in touch with her now if we hadn't needed a place to stay. She thinks we're on holiday here – don't you think she might find it just a little bit funny if we tried to land her with Lucretia? And she's a copper's daughter! That *would* be a stroke of genius wouldn't it, to let a copper's daughter in on our plans. The Crow was right about your brain – it must be concrete all the way through!"

"Well, there's Victor's mum, then. She doesn't live far. And she knows how to keep her mouth shut."

"Victor's mother?" Stella almost shrieked. "I'd rather throw her in with the sharks at Jacques Cousteau's Undersea World than leave her with that wicked old crone! We don't want anyone to have an inkling of what we're doing here and least of all her. Get this straight, Edgar – the fewer people involved in this the better. And you'd better remember that."

"All right, all right," said Edgar, and sought refuge in his beer. He was just finishing it when the Crow returned.

"She's sleeping now," he said. "You'd better get packed and on your way." He led them out to the car and watched from the doorway as they stowed their bags and the bogus policewoman's uniform into the boot of the sleek black limousine. Thoughtfully, he brought out a small gilt box from his pocket and drew forth a large black spider which wriggled and danced between his fingers. He popped it swiftly into his mouth. A stray leg remained protruding forlornly between his lips, but he gathered it in with a sweep of his tongue.

"Ugh!" said Edgar, aghast. "I wish you wouldn't do that."

"You should try it some time, Edgar," the Crow advised him. "Pure ambrosia. Off you go now – and bring the boy back undamaged."

He replaced the box in his pocket as the limousine moved away up the lane, towards Avignon, towards Paris, towards Calais, towards England, towards St Cuthbert's School and Barney Spofforth.

Chapter Two

Barney Spofforth
at School

Barney was feeling disoriented. Since arriving at St Cuthbert's School, in time for evening registration the night before the next day's lessons began, he had been surrounded by the constant sound of boys talking – that restless, ceaseless, rising-and-falling schoolroom mutter which, if you are not part of it, is the most alienating sound in the world. Once or twice he had tried putting his hands over his ears to make the hubbub more remote, but the effect was like being underwater in a dream and made him feel odder and lonelier than ever.

He was smartly dressed in a dark three-piece suit, his waistcoat neatly buttoned up, except for the last button, which his father had told him must at all times be left undone. He wore a white shirt and a blue and silver tie. The ensemble was only marred by an outsize cap that he wore, of reinforced plastic, with straps tied tightly under his chin. But that, too, was in the St Cuthbert's School colours of blue and silver.

Barney was aware that the hat made him look silly and conspicuous – the last thing he wanted – but there was nothing he could do about it. His bonnet was not there for decoration. Without it, he would be as vulnerable as a turtle without a shell.

Barney suffered from a rare congenital weakness: a form of brittle bone disease which affected his skull. The rest of him was healthy enough, but the top of his head was as fragile as an egg. A good smart tap with a teaspoon would suffice to crack it open. The specialists had said that when he was older they would be able to fit a steel plate under his scalp, making him as hard-headed as the next man – but not now, not while the bones were still growing. In the meantime, his brain was protected by a layer of bone as brittle as chalk and hardly thicker than paper; there was nothing for it but to keep wearing the bonnet.

Nobody at the school had been cruel to him so far but his strange headgear attracted many strange stares. Perhaps the teachers had warned the other boys beforehand for he was not pestered with any enquiries about it. He had been placed in a second year form called, for some reason, the Remove, under the tutelage of Mr Pargeter, a thin, pale, prematurely bald young man whom nobody took much notice of. There were some thirty boys in the Remove and they all knew each other from last year. Their talk was full of ancient anecdotes and allusions that Barney didn't understand, though he smiled whenever everybody else laughed to show that he was prepared to join in.

It had been his father's idea to send Barney to boarding-school. It would make a man of Barney, he said. Besides, now that his soup-making had made him a rich man he wanted his son to consort with the sons of other rich men – although since he had picked the cheapest boarding-school he had been able to find this wasn't very likely. Barney's mother had been less whole-hearted about the idea. She thought that Barney at thirteen was rather too young to be made a man of and was in constant dread about the state of his head. However, on the understanding that Barney was to be excused all rough games she had finally given in.

As for Barney himself, he wasn't sure what he thought. A part of him was panic-stricken. Stories he had read or heard about boarding-school haunted him: boys who were roasted over slow fires in the Common Room, flicked with wet towels in the changing-rooms, made to undergo unspeakable initiation rites in the dormitory or flogged by the teachers for misconstruing their Latin. Of course, he told himself, that sort of stuff didn't happen any more, all that *Tom Brown's Schooldays* business, it belonged to the nineteenth century. But the real terror remained: the terror of having to meet seven hundred new faces and find a way to get on with their owners.

Barney's parents had sheltered him a good deal from life until now. This was partly on account of the fragility of his head, but also because they themselves were nervous people who regarded the world around with distrust. Mr Spofforth would certainly have led a quiet and totally uneventful life had it not been for his strange genius at soup-making, and his wife was even shyer than he was (which was why he had married her). Yet there was a part of Barney which rebelled against all this feather-bedding, rebelled even against having to wear his protective helmet. He craved adventure. Going to St Cuthbert's could certainly be viewed as an adventure, and when he was able to view it in this light the prospect excited him. Thus he vacillated between bravery and cowardice; and curiously, it was his father's attempts at encouragement which intensified his cowardice, while his mother's evident nervousness about the whole thing fed his bravery.

After supper the boys gathered in the Remove Common Room, a large area with a dirty grey carpet, fluorescent lighting, a table-tennis table at one end and a television set at the other. They were allowed one hour of recreation before bedtime. Barney wondered whether he should introduce himself to his form-mates. But what would he say? "Hello, I'm Barney Spofforth"? To make this as a general announcement would surely lead to general laughter; but to go up to them one by one and shake hands like a visiting member of the Royal Family would be ludicrous.

In the event the decision was made for him. One of the boys detached himself from the group he was with and strolled over in his direction. Barney had already noticed him; he seemed to be the class wit, always ready with a smart, cutting retort or a cynical quip. He wore glasses and had an impish, quizzical face. His name was Jeremy Carver.

"You're Spofforth, aren't you?"

"Yes, that's right."

"Spofforth of Spofforth's Soups?"

"Yes, that's right," said Barney again, mildly surprised that he should be so famous. "Have you – er – tried it?"

"He wants to know if I've tried it!" said Jeremy, provoking giggles from those nearby.

"No, no, the soup, I mean. Have you tried the soup?"

"Oh, the soup! Yeah, I've tried it."

"And did you like it?"

"It was absolutely disgusting."

Barney knew that this was unfair – his father's soups were delicious – but there was no appeal against the shout of laughter which arose.

"Your dad must be rich, then," Jeremy went on.

"He's – he's well off," Barney admitted.

"What's he doing sending you to a dump like this, then?"

"Oh," said Barney. "Is it a dump?"

"He wants to know if it's a dump!" said Gregory Snood, a friend of Jeremy's. He was slightly less popular than Jeremy and so his effort provoked slightly less laughter.

"Yeah, it's a dump all right," said Jeremy. "Sometimes people bring their rubbish here and drop it in the quad. They think we're the municipal rubbish tip."

"Yes, and don't stand outside the gates on Thursday morning. Otherwise the dustmen will carry you away!"

"If it wasn't a dump," finished Jeremy, "people like us wouldn't end up here."

"Ha, ha," said Barney politely, hoping he wasn't being impolite by mistake. This level of banter was going to be hard to keep up with. It seemed that a joke was required every thirty seconds or so. Still, at least no one had attacked him yet, or tried to take his bonnet off.

But the ordeal, if ordeal there was to be, might

well come in the dormitory after lights-out. Barney reached into his pocket and clutched the little carved wooden duck there. He had kept it as a bedside ornament for years and had brought it along with him thinking that it might make him feel more at home amid the alien surroundings of St Cuthbert's.

When they were ushered up to their dormitory by Mr Pargeter at nine-thirty, Barney was relieved to see that of the eight beds the one allocated him was nearest the door – well-positioned for an escape, should that prove necessary. His second reaction was one of dismay as he realized that it only had one pillow. His parents, he knew, had written to the school stating his requirements. Somebody had slipped up. What was he to do? Mr Pargeter had already left.

"Er – excuse me?"

"What is it?"

"Do you think there are any more pillows? That I can, well, borrow?"

"What do you want pillows for, Spoffo?"

"He wants something to cuddle."

"You can cuddle me if you like!"

"No, cuddle me!"

"No, me!"

"Cuddle me, Spoffo."

Barney gave a sickly grin. "No thank you," he said. "The trouble is, you see..."

"What's the trouble, Spoffo?"

"Tell us what the trouble is!"

"We want to know about the trouble!"

"I – I usually take my bonnet off at night. To – er – let my head breathe."

"Yes, you wouldn't want your head to suffocate," said Jeremy Carver gravely.

"So – so I have to have extra pillows for protection," said Barney when they had stopped laughing.

"Better go to Matron, then."

"Matron? Er – where is she?"

"Down the pub!"

Barney waited for the laughter to subside. "No, but seriously..."

"Oh, *seriously*," said Jeremy Carver. "If it's *seriously* then that's *different*. Her room's straight ahead at the end of the corridor. Just knock and walk straight in."

"Thank you."

Barney traipsed down the corridor in his bare feet, tapped at the door that faced him and pulled it open. A higgledy-piggledy array of mops, brooms and buckets confronted him. From the dormitory, that already detestably familiar shout of laughter came echoing down the corridor.

He found Matron eventually and returned to the dormitory clutching three pillows. The other boys watched critically as he arranged them into a nest where he might safely cradle his head, cushioning it against the shock of any sudden tossing or turning. He placed his wooden duck on the bedside, turned out the lights and got into bed.

"Hey, Spoffo!" He heard the voice of Gregory Snood. "What happened to your head?"

"Well, nothing happened to it, exactly."

"What's wrong with it, then?"

"I – I've got a weak skull. I was born like it."

"That was a bit of bad luck!"

"Do you have to wear that stupid hat – that nice hat, I mean –" general laughter again – "do you have to wear it all through the day?"

"Er – mostly," said Barney. "I take it off to wash my hair."

"He takes it off to wash his hair!" said Jeremy Carver. "The boy's a genius!"

Barney closed his eyes and tried to ignore their laughter. For some time as he lay there, courting sleep and failing to win it, he heard voices whispering and sniggering. He pressed the pillows closer to his ears and forced himself not to listen.

At length the room fell silent. Everybody else was sleeping; but Barney lay awake for a long time, staring into the darkness.

The first lesson next day was French with Monsieur Figgins. He insisted on being called Monsieur although he looked English to the marrow, with his pink face, blond curly hair and tweed jacket. He spoke French with what even to Barney's untutored ears sounded like a Home Counties accent. Barney had never studied French before and understood little of what the lesson was about – something to do with a family going camping, the pictures in the book told him that much – but when Monsieur Figgins said something that sounded like "Eck-ooty" and switched the tape on, he might as well have been listening to Martians.

He was resolved, however, not to lose his resolve. He wanted to do well at French. He had always had a good ear – he was good at recognizing bird calls, for example – and thought that once he had learned a few words he would be able to pronounce them rather better than the teacher. He stopped straining to understand the conversation on the tape and listened to it simply as a pattern of sounds, practising the French R under his breath. Rrrr ... rrrr ... it was rather like a motor bike starting up.

Now the tape had ended and the teacher was asking questions. Very soon he lighted on Barney.

"Er – sorry?" said Barney. "I'm afraid I don't understand."

"*Comment tu t'appelles?*"

Somehow Barney divined that he was being asked his name. Here was a chance to try out his French accent.

"Barrrney," he replied, giving it the full throttle. "Barrney Spofforrrth."

"Barrrney," came the mocking voice of Jeremy Carver from behind him. "Barrrney ... Barrrney ... Barrrney Spofforrrrrth."

And now they were all at it. "Barrrney ...

Barrrney Spofforrrth..." The echoes rang around the classroom and the accompanying giggles grew louder.

"*Taisez-vous!*" said Monsieur Figgins loudly; and Barney could see that even he was struggling not to laugh.

Barney felt his face going red. He was furious with himself. The other boys had been reasonably friendly to him that morning and he had decided that the mockery of last night had been good-natured in intent, or at least not altogether ill-natured. They were testing him; his future lay in the balance between being accepted and being a laughing-stock. The next few days, even hours, would settle it. If he kept making a fool of himself the scales could only tip one way – and a reputation as a laughing-stock, once acquired, would be all but impossible to shake off. Already it looked as though Barrrney was set to replace Spoffo as a nickname, and he had quite liked Spoffo. He reached into his pocket and fondled his duck, striving to think of something witty to say that would turn the laughter in his favour. But no words came.

Fortunately at that moment a diversion occurred.

The classroom door opened and the mild, worried-looking head of Mr Pargeter peered in.

"Is Barney Spofforth here?"

"Yes – here I am."

"Excuse me, Monsieur Figgins – could he be excused a moment? Could you come with me to see the Head, Barney, please?"

Barney rose and followed him out amid a merciful silence.

"What's it about, sir?" asked Barney as they marched down the corridor.

"Oh ... well, you'll find out in a moment. Soon enough. Keep your chin up, that's the main thing." His voice was gentle; the gentlest Barney had heard since arriving at St Cuthbert's.

The Headmaster was standing before his desk, ready to greet him. A woman Police Constable was sitting in the corner, holding her hat in her lap. She rose to her feet when Barney entered. The Headmaster placed his hand on Barney's shoulder.

"I'm afraid you must prepare yourself for some bad news, Barnaby."

"Barney," murmured Barney automatically.

"There's been an accident."

Barney felt a tingle of shock which was disconcertingly similar to excitement. It was followed by a feeling of total numbness.

"What...?" was all he could bring out.

"Involving your parents."

Barney was dully aware that he ought to start crying. At the thought a few tears prickled his eyelids.

"Are they...?"

"Police Constable Dripping will take you to see them. You're excused classes for the rest of the day, of course."

"But are they...?"

Was he going to be taken to view his parents' mangled corpses? He wasn't sure whether he fancied that.

"They're in hospital. Their condition is critical – but they're still with us, so don't give up hope."

"It's touch and go," said the policewoman, "so we'd better get moving."

She took Barney's hand in her coarse, firm grip and led him out. Barney looked up at her as they walked down to the gates. She was a tall, gaunt woman with thick black hair coiled into a bun. Her face was white and her eyes dark and deep-set, like caverns.

The waiting car was a sleek black limousine with opaquely tinted windows, quite unlike Barney's idea of a police car. As he got into the back he caught a glimpse of the driver: a huge, bulky bruiser of a fellow with a toad-like face. A sharp smell of sweat rose from him.

The policewoman pressed a switch, there was a click and Barney realized he was locked in.

The car swung out into the traffic. Barney, looking out through the window – which was only opaque from the outside – saw to his surprise that they were heading down a motorway. The ninety-five miles an hour the speedometer was showing seemed to Barney un-police-like, somehow. Was it so urgent to get to the hospital before the electro-cardiographs stopped bleeping? In that case why wasn't the siren on? He leaned forward.

"Please – where are we going?" he asked the policewoman.

"Wait and see."

"But ... my parents..."

"Your parents are all right," the woman told him. "But you're not."

She touched another button on the dashboard and a steel partition swiftly rose between the front and back seats, isolating Barney. He hammered on the partition, vainly. Through the window he saw a mileage sign. Dover 78, it said.

Chapter Three

Barney Spofforth in a Cellar

The car crunched over gravel and came to a standstill. Barney heard the door on his left side opening.

"Come out of that, young fellow," said the chauffeur, seizing his arm.

"Could I take the blindfold off now?" asked Barney. He had been wearing it for several hours and felt deprived of daylight. His captors had stopped in a motorway lay-by and tied it to him, also tying his hands behind his back to stop him taking it off. His wrists were horribly stiff. Naturally after that the journey had been a mystery tour, the more so as he had dozed through large portions of it. He knew that they had stopped at the coast because he had smelt the sea and felt its spray, but it couldn't have been a large port because there was nothing to hear except the cry of the gulls. He had been bundled into a small, creaking boat and they set off on a choppy sea crossing during which Barney felt queasy and had to be escorted to the rail, none too gently, by the bogus policewoman to be sick over the side. Then there had followed another long drive at high speed.

"You can take it off in a minute," said the woman. She led him along a rutted track and then he heard her take out a bunch of keys. A door opened and Barney found himself standing on an uneven stone floor.

The woman busied herself with the knots at his wrists and the back of his head. The blindfold was peeled away. Barney blinked and saw standing in front of him the tall, forbidding figure of the Crow.

"So here he is," said the Crow. "The little foundling."

"Who – who are you?"

The Crow merely smiled, produced a little box from his pocket, took out a spider and ate it. Barney stared in horrified fascination. The chauffeur made gagging noises.

"Don't, please don't do that," he said. "It's disgusting. It turns me up."

"Don't be absurd, Edgar. A big strong man like you frightened of spiders, it's pathetic. So, we have ourselves a house guest now," he said. "Take that ridiculous hat off him, Stella."

"No, no!" said Barney, alarmed. "I need this hat, you don't understand. It protects my head!"

"Oh, we understand all right," said Stella. "And it's coming off. You'd better keep still or I'll do you a mischief."

"You ought to know that you should remove your hat when visiting other people's houses," remarked the Crow. "Don't they teach you manners at St Cuthbert's?"

The bonnet was lifted off and Barney stood, surrounded by his abductors, with his head exposed. His scalp felt suddenly, unpleasantly cold. The Crow stared at his head like a bird eying a snail whose shell it was about to smash against a rock.

"What – what do you want with me?" said Barney.

"What do we want? We want denarii. Lots of them. Filthy lucre. Pots of it."

"He means money," Stella translated.

"But ... but I've only got one pound fifty!" This was the sum his father had given him as pocket money to take to St Cuthbert's, with the advice to "make it last".

"Not your money, you young moron," said the Crow. "Your pater's. Daddy's, that is. And here you stay until we get it. So I suggest you get accustomed to it. Take the little feller to the cellar, Stella."

"Hadn't we better give him some food?" said Edgar tentatively. "He hasn't eaten all day."

"Are you hungry?" the Crow asked.

Barney said nothing. He was famished; but they seemed to have peculiar eating habits in this house and he did not relish being offered cockroach casserole or a centipede sandwich.

Suddenly Stella laughed. "I know just the thing," she said.

Barney, motioned to a chair by a gesture of the Crow's foot, sat down and waited while Stella busied herself at the kitchen range. He tried to take stock of where he was. The room was stone-floored and wooden-walled, with the slightly forlorn air of an out-of-season holiday cottage. Outside it was dusk but through the window Barney could still make out the black silhouettes of a range of mountains in the distance. The wind was rising, gusting around the house and making the door rattle in its frame. Trees rustled; a pair of owls called to each other. Barney recognized them as barn owls and wondered fleetingly what people had called them before barns had been invented.

"Here's your supper," said Stella.

Soup. Barney took a spoonful and a familiar flavour flooded his mouth. He looked at Stella.

"Pea and ham," he said. "Spofforth's Thick Country Pea and Ham."

Stella cackled. "Your dad will be pleased to know we're feeding you well, won't he?"

"Eat the soup up, boy!" ordered the Crow. "Alas, children no longer respect their elders! That was found written on a wall at Pompeii," he added conversationally.

A lump came into Barney's throat as he thought of his parents, so far away and wondering what had become of him. They didn't know that he was sitting down to dine on their very own soup, the soup they had brought him up on, the soup that had founded the family fortune and made him a target for the kidnappers who were feeding it to him.

There was only one way to remove the lump in his throat, it seemed, and that was to wash it away with torrents of soup. He plied his spoon.

"Cellar time," announced the Crow.

Stella took him by the arm and led him through a door and down a flight of steps into the basement. She left him without so much as a good night; the door slammed, the key turned in the lock and Barney had only a bucket and a blanket for company.

The cellar was cold and damp. Barney might have got warmer by huddling into a corner but he feared that if he went to sleep and woke suddenly he might tap his head against the wall. He sat cross-legged in the centre of the floor, draped the blanket over his shoulders and let his head nod forwards. He hoped that sleep would come soon. Perhaps in the morning his captors would be friendlier. Perhaps they would say it had all been a joke. Or perhaps they

37

would turn out to be the figments of a dream and he would wake up back in the dorm at St Cuthbert's.

He was surprised to find himself missing St Cuthbert's. The terrors he thought it had held seemed laughable now. He wondered how Jeremy Carver would have coped with a situation like this. Maybe he'd be scared witless? Yet it was hard to imagine the cool and ironical Jeremy being scared of anything. Barney seized on this idea as a kind of challenge. He would be as brave as Jeremy. Braver. After all, he had borne himself pretty bravely so far, and without his hat, he thought with some pride. What a story he would have to tell them when he got back to St Cuthbert's! If he got back to St Cuthbert's... But of course he would get back to St Cuthbert's. He was far too valuable for his kidnappers to harm. They wouldn't kill the goose that laid the golden eggs...

"Enjoying it down here, are you?"

Barney looked up and saw that the voice belonged to Jeremy Carver.

"They've kidnapped you too!"

"Oh, have they?" said Jeremy carelessly. There seemed to be something different about him. He wore his glasses and his sly grin as usual but his neck was greatly elongated and his body had become squat and plump with legs so stumpy they barely separated him from the floor. So Jeremy had been nothing but a goose all along! As Barney watched he squatted down and released a large, shiny, yellow egg which rolled across the stone floor.

Barney's dad pounced and held the glittering ovoid aloft. "Look at this egg!" he gloated. "I'll make some fine soup out of this!"

"I think not," croaked the Crow, who had stolen among them unperceived. "Eggs laid on these premises belong to me." He stretched out his hand to take the egg. Barney flinched as the hand drew nearer and nearer for the egg was none other than his own head . . . !

A slight noise made Barney snap open his eyes. In the door at the top of the stairs a small square panel had opened and a ghostly, white, oval face was peering through. The face regarded Barney curiously for a moment, then disappeared. The panel clicked shut – and already Barney was uncertain whether it had been part of his dream.

Chapter Four
The Girl of Barney's Dreams

Barney awoke early and found that in the grey light of morning his predicament seemed no better. It seemed worse. He felt cold and stiff and considerably less courageous than last night. As time oozed by and no one came to visit him he grew bored too, and hungry into the bargain.

In an attempt to amuse himself he began counting the stones in the wall. They were mostly a good deal larger than standard bricks but they were not all of a size and the rows they were laid in were not quite straight. Their total, therefore, could not be reached by a simple multiplication of rank and file – they had to be counted individually and the sum kept coming out differently. On the whole, Barney decided, there were six hundred and four of them, at least that was the answer he arrived at most frequently, but he could not be certain and didn't wish to be, for then the game would be over for good.

Still no one came. Barney invented some variations to spin the counting game out: how many squares of four stones were there? Of nine? Of sixteen? And how many triangles of three, of six, of ten stones were there?

Barney was just getting tired of the game, and had discovered that even if he closed his eyes he could still see the stones, when the door opened. Stella marched briskly down the steps holding a bowl of cold spaghetti.

"Lunch," she said, and plonked it down in front of Barney.

Then her eye caught the bucket, which Barney had had no option but to use that morning. Her nose wrinkled.

"Ugh!" she said. "Well, I'm not emptying that. Edgar can do it later. Ugh!"

Barney squirmed with embarrassment. The woman's reaction was monstrously unfair – after all, why hadn't they let him use the toilet? He did not, however, dare to point this out. Instead he asked meekly: "Please – how much longer are you going to keep me here?"

"Why?" said Stella in mock astonishment. "Don't you like it here?"

"I want to go home!" said Barney, unable to keep the quaver out of his voice.

"Oh dear, what a heart-rending little plea! You'd better not make me cry, or my contact lenses will fall out!"

"You're – you're breaking the law!"

"I'll break your head if you don't shut up," she replied, and her harsh cackle grated on his ears. She exited, locking the door behind her.

How much longer *would* they keep him here? As he despondently ate his spaghetti, Barney wondered whether they were making plans about him upstairs at that very moment.

They were.

"When are you going to get in touch with the kid's parents?" Stella asked the Crow as she ladled Spofforth's Barley and Venison Broth into his waiting bowl. They were sitting down to lunch. Lucretia was up in her room, attempting to read, at her father's orders, Caesar's *Gallic Wars*.

"Soon," said the Crow, "but not quite yet. We want them to get so anxious that they're actually grateful to hear from us. Let them sweat it out for a bit."

"Good idea," Edgar agreed.

"Anything to do with sweating and you're bound to approve," Stella told him meanly. The Crow laughed immoderately at this.

Edgar stared at them, deeply affronted. "I can't help it if I perspire," he said with dignity. "Some people is too polite to mention it. *Some* people is gentlemen."

"Meaning?"

"Meaning Victor Jabès, for instance."

The Crow leant across the table, took hold of Edgar's hand and, before he had time to resist, plunged it down into the bowl of piping hot soup on the table before him.

Edgar leaped up, overturning his chair, ran to the sink and stuck his reddening hand under the cold tap, cursing ferociously.

"I've warned you before," said the Crow. "It'll be your head in the soup next time."

The Crow nursed a profound and bitter resentment against Victor Jabès. They had met shortly after the Crow and his followers had moved to Paris, finding England a little uncomfortable for their operations just then; they had fallen in with Jabès and agreed to team up. The Crow liked the idea of having a French partner. It made him feel like an international criminal.

They had got on well at first. Jabès was polite and seemed impressed by the Crow's knowledge of classical civilizations. But tensions made themselves felt. The Crow was accustomed to lead, and Victor treated him like a species of lieutenant. He was also amused by the Crow's soubriquet and insisted on calling him "Monsieur Corbeau". To make matters worse, Edgar conceived a dog-like respect for the fat, bearded Frenchman with his sly politeness and his air of superiority. Solely to annoy the Crow, Victor invited Edgar down to Provence to spend a weekend with his old mother on one occasion.

The first job they collaborated on was a bank robbery. It passed off successfully but the share the Crow and his team received was less than a quarter of the proceeds. "I have my overheads to consider," explained Jabès. Stung, the Crow determined to be in charge of the next operation and offered up his kidnapping plan. Victor was having none of it – only because he hadn't thought of it himself, the Crow knew, but Victor claimed with sickening hypocrisy that his conscience was against the idea.

"The little children ... the poor little innocent children ... it is not just to bring them into danger. There are some things one cannot do. You may call me a sentimentalist, if you wish."

The Crow called him a lot of worse names than that. But eventually he had to acquiesce to Victor's own plan, the robbery of a jeweller's shop in the Rue de Rivoli where, it seemed, a sales assistant had been rude to Jabès.

As a result the Crow found himself on the receiving end of the worst double-cross he had ever suffered. After assisting in the planning, visiting the shop (and buying cuff-links he didn't want) to check the layout of the premises, advising on how to neutralize the alarm and stealing a car for the get-away, he arrived at the rendezvous only to find that Jabès had nipped in ahead of him and looted the place already. There was nothing left in the window but a scrawled message on a piece of paper. "The early bird catches the worm," it said.

The Crow vowed that when he caught up with Jabès he would hitch him to the back of his car and drag him round and round the Place de la Concorde like Achilles dragging Hector's body around the walls of Troy behind his chariot. But since then they had not met. Perhaps Jabès had left Paris.

The Crow decided to leave it too. Stella's ex-sister-in-law, Annick, had a holiday cottage in the South of France. Though they didn't get on, in fact had not spoken for years, when Stella contacted her and asked if they could have it for a few weeks she agreed – perhaps out of sentiment for Lucretia, whom she'd been very fond of as a small child. The Crow was delighted. It made the perfect base for their kidnapping operation. "And won't Jabès feel sick," the Crow liked to say, "when he hears we've netted two million pounds without him!"

"What are you doing, Edgar?"

It was the voice of Lucretia, who had crept downstairs.

"Burnt my hand," said Edgar sourly.

"What are you doing down here? You can't have finished the Caesar yet!"

"No, I haven't," said Lucretia. "It's boring."

"Boring?" said the Crow angrily. "You've used the wrong word there. I think you meant to say 'interesting'. Now get back upstairs and get on with it. Otherwise it'll be Thucydides instead!"

Lucretia sulkily returned to her room. On the way, unperceived by her father, she cast a mutinous glance at the cellar door.

It was too dark now for Barney to play the stone-counting game. Instead he was listening out to identify nightbirds calling. He had logged a Scops Owl and a nightjar plus those barn owls again. He had also heard a fox barking and the plaintive stridulation of the cicadas could always be heard. The mournful night-sounds deepened his mood of gloom. He put his hand in his pocket and caressed his wooden duck. How much longer would he be confined here?

There was a rattling at the door. Barney squeezed his duck. He dreaded to think why the fearsome, spider-eating Crow should come to visit him at this hour. Not that Stella would be any better. Perhaps because she was a woman and he expected gentler treatment from her, there was something peculiarly shocking in her malice towards him. Of the three of them Barney much preferred Edgar. Despite his brutal appearance and powerful body odour, there was an air of the underdog about him that Barney couldn't help but find appealing. When he'd been in earlier that evening to empty Barney's bucket and bring some more food he had stayed to exchange a few civil words, and though the civil words were ludicrously inapt, of the "Turned out nice again" variety, Barney appreciated the thought.

Which of them was it this time?

It was none of them. The door opened and shut quietly and a little, dark figure tiptoed down the steps towards Barney. He had thought the night completely black but a little starlight must be filtering in through the ventilation grille, for he was able to see that the dark figure had a pale face.

"You're the girl in my dream!"

"Ooh, the girl of your dreams!" the face giggled. "That's what I call a welcome."

"But – but who are you?"

"Lucretia," said Lucretia.

"Have they kidnapped you too?"

Lucretia laughed. "Feels like it sometimes. Dad makes me sit up in my room all day trying to read nasty Virgil and Suetonius. No, I'm the daughter."

"Do they know you're down here?"

"Ha! They'd kill me if they did. I'm not supposed to know anything about you."

"So . . . how did you find out, then?"

"I keep my ears open," said Lucretia. "Not much gets past me."

"But how did you get in? I thought that big fat man was on guard outside."

"Edgar? He's been sitting there drinking bottles of beer all night. I just waited till he went to the bog. I got hold of the spare key. That's what comes of being the daughter of a Master Criminal."

"Ye-e-es . . ." said Barney, not quite sure he liked the way she sounded so proud of it. "Still . . . even if he is a Master Criminal, that doesn't give him the right to go around kidnapping people, does it?"

"Doesn't give him the right to go around kidnapping people," said Lucretia in a kind of namby-pamby, all-purpose mimicking voice. "Isn't it

49

shocking, the nasty man has broken the law. Deserves a smack on the bottom." She must have inherited her sarcasm from her mother. "Anyway, if I were you I'd be enjoying it. It's an adventure, isn't it?"

"You don't think they'll – do anything to me, then?"

"Not if your dad pays up. But otherwise . . . ooh, I wouldn't like to say. He's a terror, my dad. So's my mum, if it comes to that."

"Yes, I know," said Barney feelingly. He wondered whether Lucretia loved her parents. But it was too personal a question to ask on such a short acquaintance. Instead he asked: "Your dad – why does he eat spiders?"

Lucretia laughed. "Oh, he fooled you, did he? He doesn't eat them really. He has them specially made out of liquorice. He does it to frighten Edgar. Edgar's an arachnophobe. That means he's frightened of spiders."

"Yes, I know."

"Ooh, you are clever, aren't you? Is it true you've got a weak head?"

"Yes, I've got a very weak head. I have to be careful."

"Well, I've got something wrong with me too, and so do I have to be careful," said Lucretia as though to say "One–all". "I've got lupus erythematosus. I suppose you know what that means too."

"Er – no, I don't."

"It means I'm allergic to sunlight. I can't go out in the daytime, unless it's cloudy."

"What happens if you do?"

"Ooh, all my skin would bubble up and then I'd faint and probably die."

"Sounds serious," said Barney, not knowing what else to say.

"Oh, it doesn't bother me," said Lucretia with a toss of her head. "I prefer the dark, anyway."

"Do you?"

"Much better than the nasty old sunlight. More interesting."

Barney realized he was smiling. For the first time since his kidnap – since he had been sent to school, in fact – he felt happy. Lucretia's presence in his cellar stimulated him. How nice she was! He had a sudden urge to give her a present. He took his duck from his pocket and pressed it into her hand.

"What's this?"

"A present. A little duck."

"A lovely little wooden duck! Thank you, Barney-boy!"

"I've had it a long time."

"Then here's something for you," said Lucretia, making a decision. "I've had this a long time too."

Barney curiously examined the tiny silver brooch she had given him.

"Is it a dog?"

"No, it's a wolf. Like me, you see – I'm like a werewolf, I can only go out at night. My Auntie Annick gave it to me when I was little. Put it on."

"But if your parents see it, won't they know...?"

"No, they've never seen it. It was a secret present. She gave it to me when I was about four. We haven't seen her for years – Mum and Dad quarrelled with her after my Uncle Geoff died. They never liked her anyway, because she's French and a copper's daughter. But she was a lovely woman. I still miss her. This is her cottage, you know. But I don't expect she'll visit us. Don't even know if she still lives in France."

"So this is France, is it?"

"Yes, you brainy Barney, it is."

"Really? Where in France?"

"Somewhere far away from prying eyes. You must think I'm a bit of a moron if you think I'd tell you that. Then you'd be able to tell the cops and help them trace my mum and dad. That would be really clever of me, wouldn't it?"

"I – I only asked."

"I don't want them to go to prison, you know – even if they are my parents."

That was a curious way of putting it, thought Barney. So perhaps she didn't love them after all.

From outside in the passage there came the faint sound of a chair scraping on the stone floor.

"That's Edgar getting up to go to the bog again. I'll have to go now."

She skipped nimbly to her feet.

"Thanks for this beautiful wolf," said Barney. "I'm touched."

"Thanks for the duck!"

"You will come and see me again, won't you?"

"Maybe! Maybe not!"

She bent down and applied a swift kiss to Barney's cheek, and was up the stairs and out of the door like a little vanishing imp. Barney felt the imprint of the kiss lingering on his cheek for a long time after the door had closed behind her.

Chapter Five

A Ransom Demand

The cellar door opened and the morning sunlight came streaming down the steps.

"Master Barney Spofforth?" came the Crow's strident tones. "Kindly oblige me by stepping this way. The morning is here and there's work to be done. Carpe diem! – That's Latin for 'Seize the day'," he explained. "Or, more colloquially, let's get on with it."

Barney ascended the steps. His three captors were waiting for him in the kitchen. The Crow surveyed him sardonically, took a spider from his little box and munched on it. Barney noticed how he twisted it between his fingers to produce an illusion of movement.

"Sit there."

Barney sat down.

"Looks a bit of a mess, doesn't he?" said the Crow critically. "Perhaps we should tidy him up a bit."

"Perhaps we should comb his hair – with the leg of a chair!" cackled Stella.

"There's no need for that!" said Barney, alarmed. He gingerly smoothed down his hair with his fingertips. Stella and the Crow laughed.

"Oh, leave the kid alone!" said Edgar.

The Crow fixed him with an icy stare.

"You'd better watch your mouth, Edgar," he said. "Or I'll push some spiders in it."

Edgar writhed uncomfortably and looked at the floor.

"Right," said the Crow at length. "We'll move on. Camera, Stella?" He took the camera, positioned Barney in the viewfinder. "Say cheese!"

"Cheese," mumbled Barney.

"And – click!"

The camera whirred and ejected a damp print of Barney's wan smile. The Crow looked at the picture in satisfaction.

"We shall dispatch this to your pater," he told Barney, "with our demand, and should soon be in receipt of ransom. If all proceeds according to plan you will be free by the end of the week."

"That's good," said Barney sincerely.

"Yes, but only if all goes well, you understand," cautioned the Crow. He picked up the soup ladle that was lying on the table. "If not ... soup ladle, Barney's head. Barney's head, soup ladle. You two will find yourselves getting better acquainted." He took a couple of practice swings through the air with the ladle. "Now return to your cellar. And don't look so sad. Do you know what happened to Prometheus?"

"No."

"He was chained to a rock as a punishment for stealing fire from the gods and a vulture came to peck his liver out every day for all eternity. So you've got it easy, really, haven't you?"

The letter, when it arrived, was a positive relief to Barney's parents. They had been living on their nerves ever since St Cuthbert's had contacted them, after Barney had failed to return and it was

57

discovered that none of the hospitals in the locality had any record of the Spofforths' admission, nor the local constabulary any record of a WPC Dripping.

Mrs Spofforth's immediate reaction was to blame her husband. "I told you we shouldn't have sent him away to that school! It would make a man of him, you said. I knew it, I knew all along it would end in disaster!"

"How was I to know, woman?" Mr Spofforth defended himself. "It didn't say anything about kidnapping in the prospectus, did it?"

He was not accustomed to being criticized by his wife and he didn't enjoy it. Her evident panic made him all the more determined not to reveal his own worry. "There's no point in getting hysterical," he advised her in his lordliest manner. "That won't help matters."

But Mrs Spofforth refused to be placated and followed him from room to room of the great bare house, hectoring him incessantly.

It was five days before word from the kidnappers arrived.

Barney's father knew what the letter was as soon as it landed on the mat. The address was typed and the French stamp postmarked from Paris. He slit it neatly open with his stainless steel letter-opener and read it aloud.

"My dear Spofforths: greetings, or Salve as they said in Ancient Rome! The three Fates, Clotho, Lachesis and Atropos, who weave men's destinies, have introduced a new thread into your son's life; and stand ready to cut him out of the pattern altogether if you refuse to play the part allotted to you. Like Helen of Troy, your son has been abducted; though there the parallel terminates, for you can ensure his safe return by collecting two million pounds sterling in used fifty pound notes and putting it all in a nice big bag – or two bags, if necessary.

"You will presently receive further instructions as to when and where to deposit the ransom. I should mention that if you inform the Myrmidons of the Law of the contents of this letter, the punishment will be visited on the head of your heir; and that punishment may well be *capital*.

"Ave,

"A Master Criminal."

Mr Spofforth crumpled up the letter and flung it to the parquet floor. "Bandits!" he said.

Barney's mother picked it up, uncrumpled it and scanned the contents through again. "Oh, good gracious, two million pounds! But you've got it, haven't you, Arnold? You've got the money?"

Mr Spofforth looked cagey. The exact extent of his fortune had always been something of a secret.

"Possibly," he conceded. "But we're not paying it. Don't you see that's exactly what they want us to do?"

"Of course it's what they want us to do! That's why they asked us to do it! We've *got* to pay ... we can't risk..."

"If they ask for two million, they'll take one," said Mr Spofforth sagely. His business habits had rendered him a compulsive haggler.

"But Barney's head – we've got to do what they ask..."

"I never do what criminals ask, on principle," replied Mr Spofforth. He was a timid man, but like many timid men he had a streak of stubbornness in him. He was proud of the fortune he had amassed through his own thrift and industry, and the idea of handing a great chunk of it over to criminals – people who deserved punishment, not reward – was bitterly repugnant. And safe in his high-walled mansion it was easy to defy them.

"But what about our son? How are we going to get him back if you don't pay?"

"We'll get him back, don't you fret. I'm not going to be outwitted by a bunch of rascals like this lot. You know me better than that."

"How? What are you going to do?"

"I'll make them an offer and we'll come to terms. I'm no soft touch when it comes to bargaining, you know. And when we've got Barney back I'll pursue them – I'll pursue them," he blustered, "to the ends of the Earth! I'll make soup out of them!"

"You don't care – you don't *care* about Barney – all you care about is money!"

"Of course I care about Barney!" shouted Mr Spofforth. "It's the boy's inheritance I'm trying to safeguard, can't you see that?"

"His inheritance won't do him much good if his head's caved in!" said Barney's mother, beginning to cry.

"There's no need to cry," Mr Spofforth told her irritably. He attempted to put his arm around her but she shook him off.

"How can you make them an offer anyway? You don't even know their address!"

"I'll hire a detective."

"But we can't fool about with detectives! The police told us to contact them as soon as we heard anything. Let's leave it to them."

"I see no need to involve the police. This is between me and those bandits," said Mr Spofforth. As he said it he saw himself as a lone hero, a virtuous man battling single-handed against the forces of evil. The idea of hiring a private detective appealed to him. In detection work, as in education, Mr Spofforth believed, you got what you paid for. It might save him a million in the long run.

"The kidnappers told us not to inform the police," Mrs Spofforth reminded him cannily.

"Precisely. And then?"

"I thought you never did what criminals asked?"

"Hmmm." Mr Spofforth considered for a while, then crossed the room and picked up the phone. "Hello, police?"

It was a long and lonely day for Barney. The seconds staggered past like arthritic ants. He hoped that Lucretia would come to call on him that night. An idea had begun to form in his brain.

To make the time pass he was playing a new game – the fantasy game. In the fantasy game he envisioned himself as the hero in a succession of perilous adventures – except that they were not perilous, for in them he was invulnerable, able to dive through windows or out of moving cars or suffer thunderous clouts to the skull without so much as a headache as a result. His enemies – sometimes the Crow or Stella, sometimes, for some reason, Jeremy Carver – were powerless to harm him, at least in the waking stage of the game. But now he was passing into a doze – he was losing control of the game – a sense of imminent danger and death hedged him around, pressing closer and closer...

He came to with a start, his heart palpitating, and snapped open his eyes – to see the welcome figure of Lucretia gliding down the cellar steps towards him.

"Brought you some bread and cheese," she whispered.

"Oh, thanks!" Barney seized on the food gratefully. They never gave him quite enough to eat here and he had been hungry ever since he arrived. He munched in silence for a while, wondering how to bring the conversation round to his idea.

"Do you speak French?" he asked.

"*Mais oui, monsieur, je parle très bien français.*"

"So you do?"

"I've picked up a bit since I've been here," said Lucretia carelessly.

"Useful," commented Barney. Perhaps he should unveil his idea right now? Or would that be too impetuous? After all, he had not known her very long and if she said no he would feel crushed. She might stop visiting him. On the other hand if she said yes he would be filled with delight. And the fact that she visited and brought food to him proved that she was well-disposed. He decided to plunge.

"I – I bet you've got the key to unlock the front door, haven't you?"

"Maybe. Maybe not."

"You could get me out of here then, couldn't you? Help me escape!"

As soon as the words were uttered Barney knew they were a mistake. He felt rather than saw Lucretia stiffen.

"Oh, so that's it, is it?" she said. "That's what you

want from me. It's not enough that I bring you bread and cheese – risk a terrible row by coming to see you – now you want me to do the dirty on my own parents. You want me to betray my own mum and dad. You want me to do them out of two million quid!"

"Is it as much as that?" said Barney, impressed despite himself.

"And what about me? Have you thought of me? If I help you escape you'll run off home to Mummy, but where will I go? I'd really be the favourite daughter then, wouldn't I? I couldn't come back here, they'd kill me. But you didn't think about that, did you? You're a selfish little boy. I don't like you any more."

"I'm sorry," said Barney miserably. He felt flattened, as though a huge cartoon foot with the word "Rejection" written on it had stamped on him. They had been getting on so well before. Now he had spoilt everything.

"I didn't mean to offend you," he said. "Only it's horrible being stuck down here. It's lonely. I want to get out."

"Oh, and I suppose you think my life's a bowl of

cherries, do you, trapped here in this nasty cottage with a pile of nasty old Latin books and the sun blazing away outside? Oh, yes, I'm having a whale of a time. The night-life here is so wonderful. There's the moon and the stars, and last night I saw some moths! Night-life!" she went on bitterly. "That's all I ever get to see."

"There, there . . ." said Barney uncertainly.

"And I thought you could be my friend!"

"But I am your friend!" said Barney, seizing on this. "I'm your very good friend. I only mentioned that about escaping because I thought – well, I thought it would be an adventure, like you said. It's not *you* I want to escape from."

"There's Edgar getting up. Time to go." And without another word she slipped out of the door. No kiss, this time.

Chapter Six

Mickie Trickie,
Private Eye

In Mr Spofforth's view, the police were doing a far from satisfactory job. They were sympathetic, of course, a fact which seemed to impress Mrs Spofforth inordinately, but what use was sympathy? Sympathy cost nothing. Detective Inspector Belcher, who was in charge of the case, had explained that they were pursuing all the usual lines: they were checking their records for all possible candidates with previous form; they had alerted the French police and passed on a description of Barney; the letter had been fingerprinted and analysed by forensic experts. But what was the result? There wasn't one. Belcher claimed that they would have more to go on when the ransom demand proper arrived.

"It's by the money that we'll trace them, you see, sir," he told Mr Spofforth.

"You mean I've just got to hand the money over?" said Mr Spofforth incredulously. "It seems to me I've wasted my life in soup. Seems to me there are easier ways to get rich."

"It's better at this stage to comply with the kid-nappers' demands. Don't forget the boy's safety may be at stake."

"Oh, but we can't forget that for a moment!" Mrs Spofforth burst out.

"Of course not, we never forget it," said Mr Spofforth. "But I must say it comes as a surprise to me to find a top-ranking police officer recom-mending me to feather the nests of known crim-inals."

"We'll recover the money when we catch the criminals, of course, sir."

That was all very well to say, thought Mr Spof-forth; but it wasn't Detective Inspector Belcher's money that was being handed over.

"He seems to think that money grows on trees," he grumbled to his wife.

"Well, money's made of paper, isn't it? And

paper's made from wood. So in a way it does grow on trees."

After that, Mr Spofforth decided it was not worth pursuing the conversation. He said nothing more to his wife about his plan to engage a private detective. She wouldn't understand.

But when he came to research into the matter, Mr Spofforth found he didn't understand either; didn't understand how reputable detective agencies, while able to offer no guarantee of ultimate success, were able to charge such extortionate rates. One after another they proved immune to his powers of bargaining. Mr Spofforth was on the point of giving it all up as a bad job and leaving the enquiry in the hands of the police – after all, he paid their wages too, through taxes (as he had frequently pointed out to the Inspector) – when a lucky find made him change his mind once again.

It happened on his weekly trip to the newsagent to buy his weekly ounce of pipe tobacco. He was idly scanning the hand-printed cards in the window advertising second-hand vacuum cleaners, children's bikes and massage services when it jumped out at him: a neatly-written card at the foot of the window which read: PRIVATE DETECTIVE WITH FLAIR FOR INVESTIGATION, EXTRAORDINARY POWERS OF OBSERVATION AND PHOTOGRAPHIC MEMORY, SEEKS LINE OF ENQUIRY TO PURSUE. DISCRETION ASSURED. REASONABLE RATES.

It sounded to Mr Spofforth like just what the doctor ordered, especially the last part, which was written in red and underlined twice. He noted down the name – Mr Trickie – and the telephone number.

"I'm interviewing a man here about a job tomorrow," he told his wife. "It's for the post of chief soup-taster. So I'd appreciate it if we weren't disturbed."

When Mr Trickie turned up on the doorstep at the appointed time Mr Spofforth saw a tall, gangly figure wearing a belted raincoat and a dark trilby hat tipped low over his eyes.

"Mr Trickie?"

"Mr Mickie Trickie, yes. You can call me Mickie. If you like."

His voice was reedy and nasal and seemed to match his elongated figure.

"Well – er – you'd better come in."

Mr Spofforth led him through to the study and motioned him to an armchair. Trickie sank back into the chair as though he had just bought it and crossed his right ankle over his left knee. He took off his hat and tossed it negligently to the floor; and it was here that Mr Spofforth got a surprise. He had been expecting a much older man. At any rate, he had been expecting a man. What he had got was a boy: a fresh-faced adolescent with pimples along the line of his jaw. He could not have been older than seventeen at the outside and looked more like sixteen.

"OK," said Mickie Trickie. "Shoot."

"Shoot?"

"Give me the low-down."

"The low-down?" repeated Mr Spofforth senselessly. The young man's self-confidence unnerved him. He made an effort to seize the upper hand in the negotiations. "Before we go on I'd like to ask you a question or two. Do you have much experience of detective work?"

Mickie Trickie waved a hand in the air, implying inexpressible plenty. "Sure. Tons of it."

"Perhaps you could provide me with some references?"

Mickie Trickie shook his head. "Sorry, no way. Discretion assured, remember? I have to protect my clients."

"It's just that you seem rather..."

"Rather what?"

Mr Spofforth tried another tack. "Have you ever served in the police force?" He realized as he asked it what a ridiculous question it was. The boy was barely old enough to get into the cadets.

"Not in the police, no," Mickie Trickie replied. "I did some time in the Scouts."

"The Scouts, hmm. A most worthy body, of course, but ... to be perfectly frank I was expecting someone a little more..."

"A little more what?"

Mr Spofforth moistened his lips helplessly. If the boy couldn't see that he was too young for the job by about twenty years, how was he to tell him?

"You must realize that a very delicate and responsible commission is in prospect here."

Mickie Trickie smiled winningly. "The more delicate it is," he said, "the better I like it." Then his smile disappeared as though sponged away and his mouth became a straight, serious line. "Maybe we'd better get down to business, mister. Maybe we'd better talk turkey."

There was a tap at the door and Mrs Spofforth came in bearing a steaming mug.

"I've brought you a little something," she said to Mickie Trickie. "What do you think of that?"

Mickie Trickie took a sip.

"Very nice," he said. "A lovely drop of soup."

"So what flavour is it?"

"Oxtail?"

"It's consommé," Mrs Spofforth told him. She flashed a nervous smile at her husband as though to say, "Didn't I do well?"

"Do you think you could get out and leave us in peace?" said Mr Spofforth severely. "We're negotiating some very serious business here."

Mrs Spofforth exited, crestfallen.

"Sorry about that," said Mr Spofforth.

"That's cool," said Mickie Trickie. "When you visit a soup-maker's home, it's not too amazing to be offered a drop of soup."

"Oh, so you know who I am?"

"I've done my homework."

"That's very impressive. But ... but I have to be

completely honest with you Mr Trickie –"

"Call me Mickie."

"Mickie, then – I'm not sure you're quite..."

"Quite what?"

"Not sure if you're altogether..."

Mickie Trickie put down his soup and held up his hands in a bid for silence.

"Demonstration of my remarkable powers," he said quietly. "Please pay close attention." He placed one hand over each of his eyes. "Now, observe that my vision is totally obstructed. In other words, I'm stone blind. Description of room. Square-shaped study about five by five metres. Carpet, red with a pattern of beige fleurs-de-lys occurring at fifteen centimetre intervals. Clock with dark marble surround on mantelpiece, five minutes fast. Bookcase against right-hand wall containing fifty-two books on economics and business management and an illustrated History of Soup. Behind you is a pair of French windows containing eighteen panes of glass in total. In front of you a teak writing-desk topped with red leather, on which are placed a brown engagement diary, hemispherical paperweight with Chinese pagoda inside, blotter with pen-tray – containing fountain pen and propelling pencil in matching turquoise-blue – plus a potted geranium, just watered, to judge from the droplets in the saucer. Which is black. Oh, and there's an earwig crawling around just under the saucer. You're wearing a tweed suit with a yellow shirt and a tie made of green string. Gold-rimmed bifocal spectacles. Hair dark brown – touch of the *Grecian 2000*s, I think – straight with strands combed over to conceal bald patch on crown. Age mid-forties, say forty-six, height five foot eight or one metre seventy-one. You smoke a pipe. Your wife doesn't. She's early forties, say forty-three. Height five six or one metre sixty-five. Wearing knee-length charcoal-grey skirt, olive-green roll-neck jumper, flesh-tone tights, flat shoes with little silver buckles. She's not as fat as you but has a tendency to varicose veins..."

Now it was Mr Spofforth's turn to hold up his hands for silence, but Mickie Trickie, unable to see, carried on remorselessly.

"Out in the hall, which has a polished parquet floor, there's an alabaster bust of Beethoven..."

"Yes, that's very good," said Mr Spofforth. "Very good indeed. You can stop now. Er – quite remarkable."

Mickie Trickie uncovered his eyes. "My terms are forty pounds a day plus expenses," he said.

"Thirty," said Mr Spofforth.

"Done," said Mickie Trickie.

Mr Spofforth watched through his study window as Mickie Trickie slouched nonchalantly down the drive towards the gates.

"Did you take him on?" Mrs Spofforth wanted to know.

"Yes – er – yes, I did take him on. Young he may be," said Mr Spofforth, "but he'll go far. He's a cool customer."

He had briefed Mickie Trickie and told him to prepare for a trip to France as soon as word from the kidnappers should come through. The lad had taken it very calmly, nodding and saying "All in the day's work" in his reedy, nasal voice. Mr Spofforth would have been astonished if he could have seen the change that came over Mickie Trickie as soon as he got through the gates and out of sight.

A radiant grin spread over his face. He took off his hat and hurled it into the sky. He went running down the pavement and took a flying leap into the air. He rolled on the ground and lay on his back, arms and legs splayed out like a starfish.

"Yes!" he shouted. "That's it! I've done it! I've got a job! I'm a detective!"

Fortune had favoured the brave. He had been quaking inwardly when he turned up for the interview. Sheer bluff had carried him through. Mickie Trickie digested the important lesson: if you put on a show of confidence, others will believe you whether or not you have anything to be confident about.

What would his Auntie Meg say now? She had been nagging at him to find a job ever since he'd left school at the start of the summer. Nevertheless he sensed that this was not the kind of job she would approve of. She would say it wasn't a "proper" job. She might even try to stop him going to France.

Mickie decided not to tell her. He would say he'd got a temporary job picking grapes or something of the sort. He couldn't run any risk of her putting her size eight foot down on his dream.

To Mickie Trickie, a detective was the very archetype of a hero – a modern knight in armour. And like himself, detectives were loners. Mickie had not been popular at school. He had no close friends and was generally regarded as a bit of an oddball.

But a private detective had no need of friends. Alone he was prepared to venture down the mean streets, risking his life in his search for the truth.

From an early age, Mickie Trickie had saturated himself in detective stories. Sherlock Holmes. Hercule Poirot. Miss Marple. Lord Peter Wimsey. Philip Marlowe. Sam Spade. Albert Campion. Inspectors Wexford and Morse. He had memorized all their idiosyncrasies, their tricks of speech, habits of dress and methods of investigation. Of course, he hadn't seriously expected to become one himself when he placed the card in the newsagent's window. That had been more or less of a joke, a silly game of which he had felt mildly ashamed afterwards. It was also a result of his frustration at not being able to find what his Auntie Meg termed a "proper" job.

He was not very well-placed to do so. He had left school with a handful of feeble GCSE grades and no obvious flair for any particular job. His memory and powers of observation had not served him particularly well at school. He had felt no inclination to use them to memorize the periodic table or lists of French verbs (a pity – that would have come in useful!). He could have told you the date of birth of every boy and girl in the school; the number of classrooms and the number of tables and chairs in each; the favourite pop stars, football teams and computer games of each of his classmates; how many pairs of shoes each of the teachers owned and how many days the Headmaster wore his shirt before changing it. Unfortunately the exam board didn't offer GCSEs in any of these subjects.

Putting a card in the window had been a sort of protest at being an unemployed school-leaver, which Mickie Trickie found deeply boring and unpleasant. And now the impossible had happened! He wondered whether anyone would ever write a book about his adventures in France: *Mickie Trickie and the Case of the Kidnapped Kid*. He was now in the same league as Sherlock Holmes and Philip Marlowe and the rest of the crew – except, in fact, that he went one better, because he was real whereas they were merely fictional.

He got to his feet and dusted himself off. He had better be getting back. He retrieved his hat and put it on. Auntie Meg would be cross if he was late for tea. She was strict about that sort of thing.

Chapter Seven

The Thrill of the Chase

"So, Master Spofforth," said the Crow, standing tall before Barney. He was dressed for an outing, in a long black overcoat and black leather gloves. "If the goddess Fortuna smiles, this will be your last day with us."

"My last day?" Barney almost shouted. He had lost count of how many days he had been here now. His latest way of trying to pass the time was the classification game, in which he put all the birds, mammals, fish and plants he knew into alphabetical order. He had got as far as "hamster". It was rather a boring game.

"This afternoon we are going to pick up the ransom. Provided the money is there we shall free you on our return. If the money is not there, of course, we shall have to sacrifice you. Which would be a great pity. Sacrifice you," he mused, "like Iphigenia."

He turned and stalked out of the cellar. Left alone, Barney tried to return to his game. What came after hamster...? But he couldn't concentrate. Free today! How they would gape when he returned, fresh from his adventure, to St Cuthbert's! He imagined himself recounting the tale to Jeremy Carver and the others. "Oh, no, I wasn't scared. I just looked the kidnappers in the eye and said, 'Do your worst. You don't frighten me.' Danger doesn't bother me, you see. That's just how I am..."

There was only one drawback; the thought of it damped down his excitement at once. After he got out he would probably never see Lucretia again.

Mickie Trickie passed through Customs and Passport Control and out into the arrivals lounge at Charles de Gaulle airport. On his head he wore a sharp black Homburg which he had bought out of his expenses money and which, he flattered himself, was the last word in detective headwear. In his pocket he carried a copy of the latest letter from the kidnappers, instructing him to drop the money, packed in a holdall, at a given spot outside Paris by three o'clock that afternoon. In his right hand he carried the holdall, but it was not packed with money. It was packed with old magazines and a note offering one million pounds and not a penny more for Barney's safe return.

Mickie Trickie did not feel happy about this. The stinginess of Barney's dad shocked and distressed him. It was a shame his first ever detective job should be such a shoddy one. Mickie Trickie, an orphan brought up by a dutiful but not particularly affectionate aunt, knew what it was to feel lonely and unwanted, and his heart went out to Barney. Well, he would just have to rescue the poor kid. Rescue him and buy him lots of sweets on the way back out of Mr Spofforth's expenses money.

It took Mickie Trickie a long time to reach the rendezvous. The spot was under a bridge on a deserted road outside Aulnay-sous-Bois, a small market town to the north of Paris. He had to take the RER line into St Michel, Paris, and change there on to another RER line. Mickie had never been to Paris before, was perplexed by the transport system and spoke no French – except for totally useless words which popped unbidden into his mind, words for "rabbit", "grandfather" and "binoculars". First he got on to the wrong train, then changed to a Métro train by mistake, then he got on to the right train at last, but travelling in the wrong direction. It was half past two by the time he arrived at Aulnay and he was feeling hot and flustered.

"Cool it," he advised himself. "No need to get agitated. It's elementary, my dear Watson."

Mr Spofforth's instructions were simple. Find the spot, drop the holdall, retire to a hiding-place nearby, watch and wait, trail the kidnappers when they came to pick up the cash. But when he found the bridge Mickie Trickie began to feel worried again. The spot was well-chosen. It was surrounded by open fields; there was hardly cover for a rabbit, or "lapin" in French. True, in the distance there were some clumps of trees where he might conceal himself. But for all he knew the kidnappers had already planted a lookout and he would make an outstandingly conspicuous figure as he trudged across the fields for cover; and what if he chose to hide in the very clump of trees where the lookout was waiting? In that case his career as a detective or anything else would probably come to an abrupt end.

Even if that difficulty were got over, Mickie Trickie now began to appreciate that following the kidnappers would be far from easy. In fact, given that they would presumably arrive by car and he was on foot it would be downright impossible.

How absurd for a detective to be without a car! Detectives always had cars. Lord Peter Wimsey had one, a Daimler. Philip Marlowe drove a Buick. Inspector Morse was a Jag man. And the Saint got around in something called a Furillac. Sherlock Holmes, it was true, was car-less. But then he always seemed to be able to find a hansom cab within hailing distance.

"What am I doing here?" he asked himself aloud. Suddenly, dreadfully, his situation seemed unmanageable, his position untenable, his prospects unpleasant. He had gone too far. Swum out of his depth. Bitten off more than he could chew.

He knew the terrible loneliness of an actor who

has forgotten the first line of his soliloquy before a packed house. What was he going to *do* . . .?

"Pull yourself together, Trickie," he admonished himself. "You're on a case. This is your big break. Don't screw up."

He reminded himself once again that everybody, deep down, was quaking in their shoes as they went through life. The successful people were those who refused to let it show. Confidence and bluff could carry you through anything, just as they had carried him through his interview with Mr Spofforth.

"You'll just have to use your little grey cells," he told himself, using one of Hercule Poirot's favourite sayings.

All this while he had been approaching the bridge. It was a low bridge spanning an unimportant trickle of stream. Mickie Trickie took a few steps down the grassy declivity at the side and deposited the bag.

He set off back towards Aulnay, walking slowly, thinking quickly. The kidnappers would not arrive immediately, he guessed. They would give him a little time to get clear. How would they organize the pick-up? The lookout was probably watching him through binoculars (or "*jumelles*", in French).

When they were sure he was off the scene they would transmit some sort of signal to the driver. The lookout would advance to claim the bag, hide under the bridge and jump in the car when it came by. None of this would take place while he was still on the scene; but if he were not still on the scene he would see none of it take place.

(Mickie Trickie was quite right. At that moment Stella had her binoculars trained on him from the trees, mobile phone at the ready.)

The trick would be to be seen to depart and then return unseen. Not to the bridge itself, of course. That was asking for trouble; asking for a bullet in the guts, most likely. But suppose he stationed himself a kilometre or two down the road? Mickie Trickie did not know which direction the car would come from but he was sure of one thing: the kidnappers would not want to stop and risk a time-wasting U-turn on that narrow bridge. They would want to drive straight on, practically without a halt. Therefore, whether coming from Paris or going to Paris the car was certain to pass him. There was a risk of being recognized by the lookout, perhaps; but Mickie Trickie decided on reflection that this was a minimal risk. Few people, he knew, were as observant as he was. If he had been seen, he had been seen as a young man with a raincoat and a Homburg hat. Why should a Homburg-less young man without a raincoat, standing by the side of the road like an innocent hitchhiker, attract any attention?

The plan had its flaws. Other cars might pass and so he could not be certain of identifying the kidnappers correctly. But it was not a busy road; and besides Mickie Trickie had a sort of feeling that he would know kidnappers when he saw them. He wouldn't be able to follow them, granted; but at least he would get the car registration number, a description of the occupants and find out what direction they were headed.

It wasn't a brilliant plan. In fact it was a very dull plan. A mere scrap of a plan, a stunted dwarfish weakling of a plan. It hardly even merited the name of plan. If plans were lungs, thought Mickie Trickie ruefully, this one would have pneumonia.

But it was the only plan he had.

Having got safely out of sight past a couple of bends in the road, though still not quite at the edge of Aulnay proper, Mickie Trickie took off his hat and coat, rolled them up into a bundle which he hid behind his legs, lit a cigarette and settled down to wait. He detested smoking but all the best detectives seemed to do it. Philip Marlowe was a forty-a-day man. Hercule Poirot smoked tiny handmade Russian cigarettes. And Sherlock Holmes puffed on a filthy old pipe.

He was on his third cigarette when the first vehicle passed. An articulated lorry – a Daf, 32 tons, Mickie noted mechanically – carrying rubber goods. That was out. On his fourth cigarette a German car full of quarrelling German children came by. That was out. At his sixth cigarette, the third car drew near and stopped. The driver flung open the door and asked: "*Où allez-vous?*"

"Er..." said Mickie Trickie, trying desperately to think of somewhere the driver couldn't possibly be going. "Er – New York."

"New York?"

"*Oui. Je* go *à* New York."

The driver made a rude gesture, said something that sounded insulting, slammed the door and zoomed away. Mickie Trickie lit his seventh cigarette, screwing his face up at the vile taste of it.

The fourth vehicle approached, travelling from the bridge – and it was the one.

Mickie Trickie was sure of it.

It was a light-blue Peugeot 105, travelling fast and purposefully. There were two occupants, both in front: the passenger, a gaunt, white-faced woman with long black hair, aged in the late thirties; the driver, similar age, a big man with spiky hair, a round head and a pointy nose like a bird's. Mickie would know them again all right.

They were conversing with animated fury and didn't even glance at him. They must have already opened the bag.

The numbers on the registration plate burnt into his memory as they scorched past: 865 TV 21.

Success. But now what?

Another car approached and braked just in front of him.

"*Où allez-vous, monsieur?*"

"*Là! Là!*" said Mickie, pointing. "*Vite! Vite!*" He tried to think what "follow that car" might be in French but drew a blank. "*S'il vous plaît!*" he uttered in agony as the Peugeot dwindled in the distance. Somehow the man understood and pressed his foot on the accelerator. The Peugeot kept in sight.

The driver grinned, getting into the thrill of the chase. "*Qui est-ce?*" he asked, indicating the car ahead.

This took Mickie Trickie some time to work out, until he remembered that "*qui*" is French for "who".

"Erm – it's my grandfather," he answered. "*Grandpère. C'est mon grandpère.*"

The driver gave him a quizzical look but responded by honking the horn and pressing harder on the accelerator. Now they were gaining ... the thrill of the chase ...

But the thrill of the chase didn't last long. They were soon in the centre of Aulnay and there, as they rounded a corner, was the Peugeot standing parked and empty at the kerb. They must have had a second car ready.

Nothing to be done.

Mickie's driver shrugged philosophically and let him out with expressions of regret.

Failure. And now what?

*   *   *

Barney raised his head alertly at the sound of the Crow's black limousine crunching over the gravel outside. At last. In a minute or two he would be free, he was just thinking, when the cellar door burst open with such force that it smashed against the wall and rebounded. The Crow and his consort stood framed at the top of the steps.

"This is what your father thinks you are worth, boy!" said the Crow, and waved a sheaf of *Woman's Realm* magazines about before hurling them to the ground.

"He's dropped you right in it, young Barney!" said Stella, with her harsh laugh.

"Your father," said the Crow, "is a disgrace to fathers the world over. He has brought dishonour to the name of paterfamilias. Do you know what he would have been required to do in Ancient Rome following such a dishonour?"

"Don't know," said Barney weakly.

"He would have had to fall on his sword. Unfortunately he isn't with us, so we can't make him do it. That makes you his proxy, doesn't it? Stella?"

Stella handed him a glinting metallic instrument

which he raised above Barney's skull.

"No!" screamed Barney. He flung up his arms to protect his head.

"Hold his arms, Stella."

She came behind him and gripped his arms to his sides.

The Crow bent down and roughly seized a hank of Barney's hair. The scissors descended and snipped it off, scraping gently against Barney's head – enough to scare, but not to damage.

"Mind my head!"

"Mind your head indeed, I'll crush it like a hazelnut if your miserly parents don't pay up. Come on, upstairs!"

Barney was hauled up the stairs and made to sit down at the trestle table in the kitchen, blinking in the light. The Crow placed pen and paper before him.

"Now write at my dictation. 'Dear Dad, why didn't you pay the money? Now they want three million pounds instead, as a punishment for arguing. You must pay it. Otherwise they say they'll smash my head in and they mean it. Don't let me down. Love, Barney. PS Please find enclosed a lock of my hair.' That should do it," said the Crow. "And now, back to your quarters!"

"And you'll get no supper today," Stella promised him.

Supperless, Barney returned to his quarters.

Chapter Eight

A Bucket of Spiders

The dead of night. The mournful sound of a tawny owl hooting for his mate came drifting in through the ventilation grille.

"I know just how you feel," Barney told it mournfully.

There was a brief jiggling at the door and in crept Lucretia.

"Hello," said Barney dully.

Lucretia passed her arm about his shoulder and snuggled up to him.

"Careful! Mind my head."

"All right, I'm minding it!" She stroked his arm. "Poor Barney!" she said into his ear.

"You've heard, then?"

"About your dad – not paying the ransom? Yes, I heard them talking about it."

Barney was silent.

"You must be really cross with your dad."

Barney swallowed. "I'm – very upset," he said.

"Poor Barney. There, there..."

"But they won't ... you don't think they'll – do anything?"

"Well ... yes, I think they might do anything. You're not very popular, Barney-boy."

"Well, they're not very popular with me either!" said Barney, and had to stifle a sob. If he burst into tears now it would be a noisy affair and he didn't want to alert Edgar.

"There, there... Don't worry, Barney-boy. Maybe I can help."

"What do you mean?"

"Help you escape."

"But you said..."

"Oh, never mind what I said. I've been thinking it over – and I think you're right. It would be an adventure! I need a bit of excitement in my boring little life. They lug me around with them wherever they go, I never get the chance to make any friends.

No friends at all, it's ridiculous!"

"You've got me," said Barney, shyly.

"Yes, but only on my own initiative. They didn't want me to even know about you. They keep me shut up in my room reading nasty boring old Greek and Latin books. They bring me to Provence, the hottest part of France – just the place for a girl with lupus, isn't it?"

"Oh, is that where we are?"

"Yes, it is," whispered Lucretia, "and the nearest big town is Avignon. It's quite a way but if I can get you as far as there you'll be all right. Only you must promise not to tell the police anything. Stow away on a train to Calais or something. Or phone your parents. Tell them you've lost your memory."

"But what about you?"

"Oh, I'll think of a story or something. I don't care what they do to me. I hate them – especially after the way they've treated you, poor Barney-boy!"

The thought of freedom so tantalizingly close set Barney throbbing with excitement. He squeezed Lucretia's hand. "Shall we do it right away?"

"You must be patient," said Lucretia primly. "We need to be prepared. Maybe tomorrow night, if we can get everything ready."

"What do we need, then?"

"The front door key would be a good idea, don't you think? And we'll need some provisions. Food and water."

"And some warm clothes."

"And some money, if I can get some."

"And my protective bonnet. Do you know where they've put it?"

"Locked away somewhere. Don't worry, I'll find it."

"Good," said Barney. "I can't go anywhere without my bonnet!"

"And that's the lot – except that I need to collect some spiders."

"Spiders?"

"Oh, yes," said Lucretia. "We can't do this without spiders."

The day oozed slowly by. Barney watched the shadow from the ventilation grille progressing gradually across the floor. Now it was on the first flagstone

... now tickling the edge of the second ... then it was inching its way from the third to the fourth...
As it passed to the sixth it began to grow indistinct – the light was failing. Would it reach the far wall? No, it melted away into the general darkness before it could get there. Night had come again.

"Here are the spiders!" Lucretia held out the bucket for Barney's inspection. There was no doubt about it; these ones were real enough. It was too dark to make them out clearly but Barney could see a dim, swarming mass which lapped up and down the sides of the bucket; and in the quiet of the night he was even able to hear them, hear the dry whispering rustle of their little legs and bodies as they crowded and wriggled together.

"There must be hundreds!"

"Must be. I didn't count. I've been in the garden all afternoon collecting them."

"Tell me, Lucretia," said Barney after a short pause, "what are they *for*?"

"They're for Edgar."

"Edgar?"

"He's an arachnophobe, remember?"

"Yes, I know. It means he's frightened of spiders."

"He's not just frightened, he's scared witless. So next time he goes to the bog we sneak out and scatter them all over the passage in front of the door."

"And then what?"

"Don't you see? When he opens the door he won't be able to come out. I've seen him before when he's face to face with a spider, he goes all rigid. When he sees this lot he'll be petrified!"

"Yes, good joke," said Barney. "But how does that help us?"

"Because, Aristotle, that'll give us *time*. Time to get out of here, lock the cellar door behind us, get out of the front door and lock that behind us too! They won't even realize we've gone until the morning. We'll have a whole night's head start. Besides, this way's more fun."

"Why did you call me Aristotle?"

"Oh, never mind about him. Some nasty, brainy old Greek. Talking of brains, you'd better put this on."

"What is it?"

"It's a tea cosy, can't you see?'

"But what's it for?"

"For your head. That'll do, won't it?"

"What about my protective bonnet?"

"I couldn't find it. Hidden somewhere. This is just as good."

"Just as good? It's too soft. I'll be in danger! I can't go anywhere without my helmet!"

"This tea cosy is all there is," Lucretia told him flatly. "Do you want to escape or not?"

"I want to escape, but – but – oh, what the hell," said Barney. He put the tea cosy on his head. "How does it look?"

"Ooh, incredibly glamorous."

They sat down to wait; but the tension was too great to allow them to stay seated and they soon took to waiting standing up, pacing around.

"It won't be long now," whispered Lucretia. "He'd already drunk two bottles when I came by and there's half a crate under his chair. He'll burst if he doesn't go soon. We'd better be ready. I'll take the spiders. You take the keys and bag."

"What's in it?"

"Stuff. Provisions and that."

Through the door they heard the sound of foot-steps clumping away down the passage.

"That's it," hissed Lucretia. "He's off! He's round the corner... Let's go!"

Afterwards, Barney marvelled at how quickly, how efficiently their escape was accomplished. At the time he didn't marvel at all, he simply acted. It might have been rehearsed. With noiseless steps they left the cellar; Lucretia pranced down the passage to strew the spiders, while Barney re-locked the cellar door, gripping the bunch of keys tightly to prevent any tell-tale jingle. They met at the front door and it was as they were opening it that a blood-curdling yodel of horror floated down the passage-way towards them. Edgar had found the spiders.

Without a pause they passed through, deftly locked the door behind them – and there they were, out under the stars. The night breeze cooled Barney's cheek and made Lucretia's hair dance around her pallid face as, hand in hand, they made their way up the lane.

"What do you mean by this – *cacophony*?"

"Yes, what's all the racket about?" Stella rapped

out, joining him in her dressing-gown. "You've woken us up!"

"It was – spiders!"

"Are you mad? Are you insane? Spiders don't make a noise like that. Spiders don't make any noise at all. It was you, screaming your head off. Don't try and blame it on spiders."

"No, I mean," panted Edgar, "there was a dirty great swarm of spiders here – all over the floor – they was all over the place! Nearly gave me a heart attack!"

"Where are they, then?"

"They're – they're – somewhere about," said Edgar, looking wildly around. On being released from their bucket prison the spiders had scurried off in different directions, running up the walls, disappearing into fissures, seeking nooks and crannies, and by now there was not one left to be seen. The passage was bare.

"He's been drinking," was Stella's coldly-delivered verdict.

"Have you been drinking, Edgar?"

"I had a couple of bottles, but that's nothing to –"

"Drunk so much he's started seeing spiders!"

came Stella's harsh tones. The Crow marched down the passage and dragged out the clinking crate of bottles from under Edgar's chair.

"No more beer for you tonight, Edgar – or any other night. I gave you the simplest task in the world, a three-year-old child could have performed it: sit on a chair and watch a door." The Crow reached out and rattled the cellar door handle. "Still locked, thank Jupiter! But suppose it had not been? Suppose the bird had flown, and all because you were incapable of sitting on a chair and watching a door without imagining an army of spiders coming to get you? We'd have had to punish you, wouldn't we?"

"And we will punish you, if you wake us up again," Stella warned.

"Good night, Edgar."

Edgar did not reply.

"We've got to get as far as possible before the sun comes up," said Lucretia.

"Why?"

"I've got lupus, don't you remember? We'll have to hide when it gets light."

"Hide? Hide where?"

"Oh, we'll find a cave or something," said Lucretia vaguely. "A grotto."

They had already put a couple of kilometres as the crow flew, so to speak, between them and the Crow. The road wound through the picturesque countryside of Provence; hills, woods and fields all monochrome in the mysterious moonlight.

"You know the way home, don't you?" asked Barney. "The way to England, I mean."

"Oh, yes," said Lucretia carelessly. "If we stay on this road we'll get to Avignon eventually. Then there'll be signs to Paris you can follow. Then in Paris there'll be signs to Calais, I expect. Once you get to Calais you're practically home and dry."

"But we can't stay on this road," said Barney suddenly. "As soon as they find we're gone they'll be after us in the car. We'll be sitting ducks."

As if to underline his words, the sound of an approaching motor loomed up behind them.

"Quick! Which way?"

On one side of the road, a rocky, grass-tufted hill reared up towards the night sky; on the other, cultivated fields with laden vines and fruit trees in regimented rows stretched into the distance.

"Up!" said Lucretia, and the next moment they were scrambling up the slope. Their hands lost contact. In the darkness Barney lost his footing and tumbled on his hands and knees, rolled over and went helter-skeltering down the hillside.

"Barney!" Lucretia called. She skidded to a halt and picked her way to where Barney had come to rest, lying on his belly. He did not move.

"Are you all right?"

"Er – I must be," said Barney. "I can still talk."

"That was close!" said Lucretia, pointing to the granite boulder that stood three centimetres away from Barney's tea-cosied skull.

After that they proceeded with greater caution. They advanced along the side of the hill, parallel to the road below and, further away across the fields, a river.

"If we knew what that river was," said Barney, "we could follow it to its source. It might take us somewhere."

"It would obviously take us somewhere," said Lucretia. "Anyway, I do know what it is. It's the Rhône."

"Is it? Where does it come from, then?"

"Don't know."

On they trudged. The going was hard and the wind blew cold. Yet Barney wouldn't have swapped where he was and what he was doing for the most luxurious circumstances. He had always been attracted to the Great Outdoors. Now here he was, right in the middle of it. He had always felt drawn to Adventure. Now here he was, right in the middle of one. As he trekked through the moonlit landscape, dwarfed by the surrounding mountains, he was filled with a consciousness of being the hero of his own story. He turned to look at Lucretia. How nice she was!

"We'll have to look for shelter soon," said Lucretia. "The dawn's on its way. And it gets hot round here."

She pointed to the east. The sky was paling perceptibly; soon the sun would be nudging its way above the horizon. Barney surveyed the grassy incline they were trudging across. It seemed to offer little in the way of cover.

"Perhaps if we go further up the hillside," he suggested. "That looks more as if it might have a cave or two in it."

The first of the sun's rays struck them. It was going to be a nice day, if you didn't suffer from lupus erythematosus.

"Let's hurry!" said Lucretia. She was starting to feel uncomfortable, Barney saw; her breathing was quick and shallow. He delved into the provisions and stuff bag and took out the blanket Lucretia had packed.

"Put this over your head." Barney felt suddenly protective. Until now Lucretia had looked after him; now their roles were reversed. Up the hill they went, Barney with his head in a tea cosy, Lucretia with a blanket draped over hers, yashmak-style.

They found at last a rocky recess, just big enough for them both to crawl into and be shielded from the sun. It was not comfortable. The walls were damp and the flinty ground dug into them at numberless points. But worst of all was the roof. It was oppressively low, inches above their heads even when they were crouched on all fours. Barney put his hand up and felt the sharp forms of stalactites pointing straight down at his head. A teacosy wouldn't offer much protection against stalactites...

"You'd better rest your head on me," said Lucretia. "Safer that way." She arranged the blanket over both of them.

"Safer and nicer," murmured Barney. He was surprised at how warm and soft she felt. It was the first time he had ever slept with a girl. And sleep was exactly what ensued. Within seconds they had crossed the frontier into the Land of Nod.

Chapter Nine

Have You Seen This Boy?

"**H**ave you seen this boy?"

Mickie Trickie held out the photograph for the Frenchman's inspection. He was a large, bearded, bear-like man and a fat cigar smouldered in the ashtray by his elbow. He was engaged in writing a postcard; "*Chère maman*", it began. Mickie mentally filed away the details of his appearance: sixteen stone, easily, and forty-five years old. He wore a black polo-neck jumper and a cream linen jacket. Chunky gold ring on little finger of left hand. Nose small, round and smooth like a pebble washed and polished for untold aeons by the ocean.

He looked blankly at Mickie, took a sip of his cognac and turned away.

Mickie tried again, this time laboriously cobbling the sentence together in French.

"*Avez-vous voyez* – no, hang on, *avez-vous vu ce garçon?*"

"*Je regrette que non,*" was the careless reply. As Mickie moved off the man said something to the bar at large, which provoked a ripple of laughter. Since Mickie couldn't understand it he decided he could afford to ignore it. He was developing an immunity to being laughed at. This was the fifth bar he had visited that morning.

After losing the trail at Aulnay-sous-Bois he had had no option but to return to Paris. That was after all where the kidnappers' car had been heading and where their letter was posted from. The envelope had been postmarked from the eighth arrondissement, around the St Lazare area, so Mickie Trickie had proceeded thither and, without much hope but with a good deal of determination, was working his way through all the bars and cafés there, trying out on the clientele a copy of the kidnappers' photo of Barney which Mr Spofforth had given him. You never knew; somebody might have seen something.

Besides, what else could he do? He had considered, briefly, going to the French police and informing them of what he knew. The trouble was that he knew so little. He could describe the car, certainly, but since they had dumped it, it was clearly a stolen vehicle, which provided no sort of lead. He could describe the car's occupants, true, but unless they had criminal records this wouldn't tell the police much; and even if they did have criminal records – well, that would give their identities (or previous identities!) but no clue as to their whereabouts.

It was true that the police were better equipped to undertake that sort of search than he, working alone, could ever be. But to go to them now would effectively be to hand over the case. He would play no further part in it. Spofforth would curse him for a fool and a waste of money and – worse – his career as a private eye would be off to a disastrous start from which it might never recover. Detectives simply didn't go running to the police when things got difficult; that wasn't how they operated. Imagine Marlowe or Poirot or Holmes turning a case over to the police because it was too hard for them! These heroes invariably treated the police with scorn, withholding information, concealing evidence, keeping their theories secret, teasing the cops with riddles. Even Inspector Morse treated the police with contempt and he actually worked for them.

You had to play a lone hand as a detective. And that meant, when you finally cracked the case, you could hug all the glory to yourself.

Mickie moved on to the next table, where a young woman was sitting drinking a cup of coffee. Automatically, Mickie ran a noticing eye over her. Twenty-nine-ish; 172 cms-ish; light-blue jumper, dark-blue trousers. Very stylish. But shoes slightly scuffed. Blonde, frizzy hair. Green eyes. A wide, smiley mouth which gave her a somewhat clown-like appearance. She looked fit and active, probably a good tennis player.

"*Avez-vous vu ce garçon, madame?*"

"*Je crois que non.*"

She inspected the picture closely; seemed to give a slight start; squinted at it more closely still. She began to say something long and complicated in French.

"*Anglais,*" said Mickie laconically.

"English person? Well, I think I do not know the

boy. But there is something ... familiar." The woman touched her frizzy blonde hair, thinking. "If I ... remember something, if something occurs to me, can I get in touch with you?"

"Sure," said Mickie Trickie. He gave her his hotel number. "What's your name?"

"Annick," said the woman.

"Annie?"

"Annick. With a K."

"With a K. OK."

The woman got up to go and Mickie watched her leave, the hope she had briefly kindled dying away in him. She didn't really know anything. Suddenly Mickie Trickie felt weary. When he reflected on the scale of the search it was hard not to feel discouraged.

How many people were there in the eighth – supposing he restricted himself to that single district? Half a million? Would he have to interview them all before discovering a lead? Not that half a million was a static figure, of course. People were moving in and out of the district all the time. Potential witnesses must run into millions. How could he possibly hope to question all of them? It was a lifetime's work, he would have to give up eating and sleeping and going to the toilet in order to accomplish it.

And all the time that poor kid with his fragile head a prisoner of ruthless kidnappers.

Just thinking about the enormity of the task exhausted him. He decided he deserved a rest.

He went to sit by the window and ordered a *café au lait*. He lit yet another cigarette. The acrid taste filled his mouth and made him cough. He put it down, balancing it on the side of the ashtray, and watched the smoke spiral upwards. He let it burn. That way, anyone looking would assume he had a cigarette going and just happened to be between puffs. It made him look like an authentic detective without drying out his mouth or endangering his health.

He took out a book, *Maigret's First Case*, and began to read. Mickie had bought the book on purpose because Maigret was a Parisian detective.

He had not got more than a couple of pages when a shadow fell across the page. He looked up.

"Excuse me. I do not wish to disturb you," said the large bearded man with the cigar. "But may I sit down and join you for one little moment?" He spoke excellent English with only the lightest trace of a French accent.

"Sure. Be my guest," said Mickie Trickie, not letting his surprise show. Detectives never let their surprise show.

"I have been thinking, you see. The picture of the child you showed me, the little boy – it has struck a certain chord in memory. Correct me if I am wrong – but has the child recently been kidnapped? From England?"

"Possibly. Then again, possibly not," replied Mickie Trickie. Detectives never gave too much away. But though outwardly cool he was inwardly astonished. How could this bearded Frenchman know that Barney had been kidnapped? The police were keeping it out of the papers.

"I feared as much. I am a great lover of children, you see ... their beauty, their innocence, their purity. Look." He took from his wallet a collection of snapshots of simpering children and spread them out on the marble-topped table. "My nieces and nephews, they are delightful, no? Ah, children! How could anyone intend harm towards such angels?"

"It's a wicked world," said Mickie Trickie quietly. Detectives always spoke quietly; there was no such thing as a shouting detective in any of the stories he had read. The more exciting the situation got, the lower they murmured. And Mickie Trickie was considerably excited. At last he had a lead. The case was opening up right here at his table. How could this man know so much unless he had some contact with the kidnappers? Perhaps he even was one of them!

"A wicked world indeed. And I understand the poor child has a deformity, is it not? That renders the case inexpressibly pathetic. His poor, sorrowing parents! The rich, too, have their problems."

"Who told you they were rich?"

"I deduce it."

"Then here's something else for you to deduce, monsieur," murmured Mickie Trickie. "I'm on the boy's trail; you seem to know something about the boy; that means I'm on your trail. Don't move or I'll call for the gendarmes."

"The gendarmes? But why?"

"Kidnapping is a serious offence," Mickie told

him, "in France just as in England. You'd better tell me what you know."

"If you call the gendarmes you will cover yourself in ridicule. You cannot suspect me of complicity in this abominable affair?"

"I'm suspecting everyone," said Mickie Trickie, grimly.

The bearded man spread out his hands in a gesture of innocence. "I come to offer you aid and I am rewarded with suspicion," he complained. "It is true that I have a little idea – no more – of who may be responsible for this outrage. One has many acquaintances, one hears of unsavoury things. But we must proceed with caution."

"If you have information you'd better tell me what it is," said Mickie Trickie. "This may be a job for the police."

"Ah, but you do not know the French police as I do. Bureaucracy ... red tape ... forms filled out in triplicate ... if we go through these channels it may be weeks before the poor child is returned to the bosom of his family. And you, you are young, you are just starting out in business, do you not want to claim the credit for yourself? It would be a feather in your hat, as you say."

"Then tell me what you know. Who's behind it?"

"Ah, you fear that I will steal your thunder. But not at all. I am interested only in the child's safety. To you shall be entrusted the task of snatching the boy; the glory shall belong to you."

"OK. Just tell me where to snatch him from and I'll go right ahead and snatch him."

"But that is what we do not know. We must find out where these evil people are – holed out, I think you say?"

"Holed up. Holed out is a term from golf. But who are these evil people?"

"Do not be so hasty, my young friend. You wish to do everything yourself. I go to make some researches. You stay in a hotel?"

Mickie Trickie gave him the address. "But how can I get in touch with you?"

"Here: you may leave a message for me on this number if you wish to contact me."

He scrawled a telephone number on Mickie's Gauloises packet.

"But who shall I ask for?"

"Victor Jabès."

He rose from the table with disconcerting nimbleness and was out of the door before Mickie could think of another word to say.

At the corner of the boulevard Victor Jabès stepped into a phone booth. It was his habit to call his mother immediately whenever he had any interesting news to relate.

"*Allô, Maman?* Yes, your little Victor . . . I have just learned something of great importance. Do you remember the Crow family? *Oui, les Anglais.* . . . It seems they have succeeded in their scheme. . . No, I did not think they could succeed, but they have the boy, and the boy is worth millions! I do not know where they are hiding but I propose to find out. My informant? A young lad from England, a stupid boy who plays at detectives – a simple matter to lead him by the nose, he will do as I say. . . But of course I shall run no risks! It is the boy detective who will do the dirty work and then I shall relieve him of the child. But we must first find out where they have hidden themselves. . . Yes, you too should make some enquiries . . . keep open your ears . . . extend your antennae. . . I shall be in touch. . . *Au revoir, Maman! Je t'embrasse!*"

★   ★   ★

Mickie Trickie decided on another coffee before moving on. He wanted time to reflect. It was a pity that Jabès had disappeared so quickly, before he'd had time to find out more. But however you looked at it, he'd made some progress in his quest. At least he had a contact now.

What all top detectives had, Mickie Trickie knew, was a knack for being in the right place at the right time. It was a knack that couldn't be learned but without it you wouldn't get far. And Mickie Trickie had demonstrated that he had it.

He bought a postcard with a picture of the Eiffel Tower on it from the stand by the bar. He addressed it to Barney's dad and wrote: "Am in right place at right time – expect right result soon!"

Then he remembered his Auntie Meg and scribbled on the back of a Notre Dame: "Having a great time. Have picked tons of succulent grapes." That should stop her worrying.

Being a detective, Mickie Trickie decided, was child's play.

Provided that you had the knack.

Chapter Ten

On the Run

Barney awoke towards evening and noticed with a pleasurable shock the still-slumbering form of Lucretia beside him. It had been a day to remember, he thought, even though, having slept through it, he couldn't remember much about it. He wondered what Jeremy Carver would find to say if he could see him now.

He crawled to the cave mouth, keeping his head tucked down well away from those menacing stalactites, and peered out. The uplands were still lit by the rays of the declining sun but the valley below was already dark.

"Lucretia!"

He shook her gently. Her eyes flickered open.

"What time is it?"

"Time to get up."

"Oh, is it?" She hauled herself into a sitting position. "We'd better have some breakfast, or supper, or whatever it is."

They emptied out the provisions bag. The cheese had gone oozy and discoloured, and the bread so stale it showered into fragments when you bit it. They finished the feast with an orange apiece. The juice was cold and tart and left them feeling equally sour.

"If you don't like oranges you should have let me have it," said Lucretia, seeing Barney grimace. "I need a lot of vitamin C in my condition."

"Well, I need a lot of calcium in mine," Barney retorted. "You should have let me eat the cheese."

"You're welcome to it."

"Next time I'll have the cheese and you can keep the oranges."

"What next time?" said Lucretia. "There's nothing left."

The thought of walking through the night again was far from attractive. But there was no help for it. They picked their way down the slope and started traipsing along just above and parallel to the road.

"How far is it to this place?" asked Barney. "Aviemore or whatever it's called."

"It's not called Aviemore, it's called Avignon, you moron," said Lucretia. "Aviemore is in Scotland."

"Don't call me a moron, I'm not a moron."

"Oh, aren't you? I thought you were."

"Well I'm not!"

"Didn't they teach you any geography at your school?"

"They might have done, but your mum kidnapped me before they had the chance!"

"If your dad had paid the ransom," said Lucretia pleasantly, "you'd be back there by now."

"There's no need to rub it in."

"Well, don't start having a pop at me," Lucretia warned him. "If it wasn't for me you'd still be in the nasty old cellar."

"All right! How far is it, anyway?"

"Where? The cellar?"

"No! This place we're going – Avignon."

"How should I know?"

They marched on.

"It's getting cold," said Lucretia presently.

"You'd better put your blanket on, then."

"I will." She took it out of the bag and slung it around her shoulders. Barney looked at it enviously.

"I've just realized I'm cold too," he said.

"That's a shame."

"Can't I come in under the blanket?"

"No, there's only room for one."

"But that's not fair!"

"Course it's fair. I don't ask to share your tea cosy, do I?"

This stupid response disgusted Barney and he walked on in silence for a while, except for the occasional loud shiver which he hoped Lucretia was aware of. But if she was she gave no sign. The silence began to grow tense. Somewhere in the distance a nightjar chirred. "That's a nightjar," said Barney, glad to have something to say at last.

"Ooh, how interesting!"

"Yes, it is interesting."

"That's what I said, didn't I?"

"I bet you don't know the names of any birds."

"Yes I do. That one we just heard is called Gary."

"Oh, ha ha," said Barney.

They marched on.

"Is that a milepost down there on the road?"

"A kilometre-post, you mean," corrected Lucretia. "Let's go and see."

They scrambled down to the roadside. Avignon 42, the sign said.

"Forty-two kilometres! But that's miles!" lamented Barney.

"At least we're going in the right direction."

"I don't care. My legs are tired. My whole body's tired. And I've got a weak head. I can't walk forty-two kilometres."

"You don't walk with your head," said Lucretia. "Anyway, what else is there to do?"

"There's another town on the signpost, look, Tarascon. That's only ten kilometres. I'll go there. Hand myself in at the police station."

"You promised not to do that!"

"Well, I'll hand myself in somewhere else, then. The post office. But I can't walk to Avignon."

"But what about me?"

"Can't you go home?"

"But you promised to come to Avignon with me!"

"What's so special about Avignon?"

Lucretia went quiet for a while. Suddenly a loud sniff escaped her. Barney stared. The spectacle of Lucretia in tears moved him strangely. She had become a different person: a damsel in distress. He stuck his arm around her waist.

"Don't cry," he said. "Come with me to Tarascon."

"I'm sorry I was so nasty just now," sniffed Lucretia. "I've got to tell you the truth: I don't want to leave you and go back to my mum and dad. That's why I've been so ratty. And now you want to go to nasty old Tarascon!"

"I just meant, Avignon is such a long way . . ."

"So I'll have to go home even sooner!"

"But you'd have to go home in the end, wouldn't you?"

Lucretia bit her lip. "Barney?" she said.

"Yes?"

"I've had an idea."

"What's that?"

"Why don't *you* kidnap *me*?"

"How – what do you mean?"

"I can't go back to my parents now. I really can't.

126

I don't want to shop them to the cops but I can't live with them any more – and especially not after this. Take me with you!"

"You mean you want to – to go all the way?"

"Yes! Smuggle me back to England!"

The idea appealed to Barney's new-found sense of adventure immediately. Only...

"What about when we get there? What will you do then?"

"My auntie Annick lives there – you know, the Frenchwoman who gave me the brooch when I was little. Or she used to live there. I'll find her some-how. She'll take me in."

"But how will you find her?"

"We'll cross that bridge when we come to it! The big thing is to get there."

"And how will we do that?"

"No police, all right?"

"Er ... all right."

"The first thing to do is to get to Avignon. We can stow away on a train from there. I know it's a long way," she said, "but we can make it toge-ther!"

Barney looked at her. She had stopped crying

now but her eyes were still shining with tears.

"All right then. You're my prisoner. I've kidnapped you."

"You've kidnapped me."

"Shake on it?"

They shook hands.

"Let's go!"

They marched on.

Annick was of course much closer than Lucretia realized. She had left England after her husband had died and now divided her time between her flat in Paris and her parents' place in Avignon. As Barney and Lucretia were struggling over the darkening hillside together, Annick was walking along the busy Boulevard Haussman, past all the big department stores, wondering why the photo the English youth had shown her that morning seemed so familiar. Had she perhaps glimpsed the boy on a bus or in a shop? But no, it wasn't the face. . . It was some other detail. . . It was. . .

Annick suddenly halted in the middle of the crowded pavement.

It was the silver brooch the boy in the photograph

was wearing. The same brooch she had given to her little Lucretia eight years before.

But no, that couldn't be. There must be more than one brooch like that. Yet it was an unusual brooch. "*Mais comme c'est bizarre et comme c'est curieux et quelle coincidence*," said Annick to herself.

She went to a public telephone and dialled the number Mickie had given her. No, Monsieur Trickie was out. (At that moment he was wandering the streets of Paris showing his photograph to any passer-by who would stop to look.) Would Madame care to leave a message? No, no message.

After a moment's thought Annick picked up the receiver again and dialled the number of her holiday cottage in Provence.

"Yes?" said Stella.

"This is Annick."

"Oh."

"Are you enjoying your holiday there?"

"Yes, it's very nice. Thanks for letting us have it. Please don't come and disturb us."

"And Lucretia? She is well?"

"I've got to go now," said Stella. "We're very busy."

In the background, Annick heard a discordant scream of terror.

"What was that?"

"The television. There's a thriller on, two gangsters have captured a traitor and they're torturing him. It's very exciting. Goodbye."

Annick walked home thoughtfully, tousling her frizzy blonde hair.

Chapter Eleven

"A Face Like a Little Wizened Old Apple Peeped Out"

"**H**ere's a nice juicy specimen – you'll enjoy this," said the Crow. He proffered the wriggling morsel to Edgar's lips. Edgar jerked back violently but his bonds held him tightly to the chair. As his mouth opened in a gasp of terror the Crow deftly pushed the spider in. Edgar puffed and spluttered frantically, spitting out legs.

"Don't you like it?" enquired Stella. "Perhaps you'll prefer this nice speckled one."

With cruel enjoyment she forced it through Edgar's clenched teeth. Edgar's eyes were wide and staring; flecks of foam appeared at the corners of his mouth.

"He doesn't like it," observed the Crow. "That's a coincidence, because I don't like having my hostage stolen. And I don't like having my daughter stolen either. In fact, I hate it. So *where are they?*"

"I don't know!"

"Where are they, you perspiring lump of rancid lard, you sebaceous blob of fatty tissue, you oily heap of primeval ooze, where are they?"

"Tell us where they are!"

"Tell us where our daughter is, you sweaty pile of odorous excrement!"

"I don't know! I know nothing, I swear I know nothing!"

"You don't know much, I'll concede that. You're a concrete-brained cretin. But you know something about this. You were on guard when the children disappeared. What have you done with them?"

"It was the sp— the sp—"

"The spiders? The spiders opened the door for them, did they? You'll have to do better than that, Edgar. Otherwise we'll have to offer you some dessert."

"Is Jabès involved in this?" asked Stella abruptly.

The Crow clapped his hand to his brow. "Of

course! How could I have been so monumentally obtuse?"

He rounded on Edgar again and seized him by the throat.

"What has Jabès done with them?"

"Honest, boss, I don't know..."

"Don't call me boss, I'm not your boss. Jabès is your boss, isn't he?"

"No, honest, I'm not in touch with him no more, I'm not, I'm *not*..."

He began to splutter desperately as Stella tendered another spider towards his lips. "I don't even know where he is, I tell you! He was in Paris last I knew, I don't even know his address, I swear! He's history!"

"We don't believe you," Stella told him. "Still hungry?"

"Look, if I'd been in league with Victor I wouldn't have stayed here after the kids had gone, would I?" argued Edgar, desperately. "I'd have cleared off, wouldn't I?"

"You might have thought that being here would provide you with a kind of alibi – or non-alibi, rather, since the word comes from the Latin and means 'elsewhere'," said the Crow. "You might have reasoned that if you were not elsewhere we would not suspect you. And don't protest that you are too stupid to have thought of that. Jabès is not too stupid."

"But why would I need to stay here? What's the point?"

"I don't know – yet," said the Crow. "Which is why you will not be released – yet."

"But I need the toilet!"

"How very unfortunate."

The Crow rose and Stella rose with him. "I think we'll leave you now. I think we'll depart on an odyssey – that's a journey to you, Edgar – to see if we can find our absentees along the roads."

"Don't go away, will you?" said Stella, cacklingly. "We'll pick up some dinner for you on our way back."

Left alone, Edgar took several deep breaths and then began to strain every muscle in his body against his bonds. They were tightly tied – the Crow knew how to do knots – but Edgar's terror of more spiders to come lent him almost supernatural strength. His arms bulged; the veins in his temples throbbed like radioactive earthworms. The ropes did not give but the chair to which he was tied creaked protestingly. Edgar rested, then tried again. Perhaps he could break the chair apart even if the ropes held.

And if he got free Edgar knew where to run to. Madame Jabès, Victor's old mum, lived in a cottage near Tarascon, twenty kilometres up the road in the direction of Avignon.

Barney and Lucretia trudged on. Their new plan had given them new energy and put a spring in their step for a while, but now they were beginning to flag. The going was hard and being food-less didn't help. Barney remember that in tales of adventure he had read, travellers in the wild fed themselves on roots and berries; but they couldn't find any berries and as for roots, well, they had dug up a few and tried gnawing on them but found them supremely tough and indigestible.

"Must be the wrong sort of root," said Barney apologetically.

Lucretia suggested catching a rabbit. They saw several, but failed to get near a single one. Barney had had no idea that rabbits could run so fast.

Perhaps it was just as well, because they would hardly have known what to do with one if they had caught it.

"I'm fed up with this," said Barney.

"Are you? I'm having the time of my life."

She passed a hand across her forehead.

"It's – it's getting light," she said. All around colours were seeping back into the landscape. "And it's getting warm."

"We'll find some shelter soon," said Barney soothingly. "Don't worry, the sun's behind the clouds."

But just then the sun broke through the clouds and its rays burst over them. Lucretia stumbled and began panting for breath. Barney looked at her anxiously; was her skin starting to bubble up?

"Quick – put this blanket over your head! Is that better?"

"A bit – but it's so hot..."

"Look," said Barney, pointing ahead. "What's that cottage?"

Lucretia peeped through the folds of the blanket.

"It's a cottage," she said.

"I know it is. I mean, what do you think?"

"About what?"

"About knocking at the door, asking for shelter."

"How can we do that, microbe-brain? We're on the run. They'll turn us in."

"We won't be on the run much longer if we don't get out of this," said Barney solemnly. "You'll be dead. And so will I soon, from lack of food."

Lucretia hesitated.

"Just think," Barney coaxed her, "a roof over our heads. Tea and toast. A proper bed. A proper toilet!"

"Yes, but – what shall we say?"

"Some story about being lost, anything. We can be on our way again this evening – but we *must have a rest.*"

Seeing Lucretia still waver, Barney took her hand. "Anyway, you're my prisoner and that's where we're going. Come on!"

It was a typical cottage of those parts – low-built, of yellowish stone, with a bumpy red-tiled roof and shutters at the windows. A more modern note was struck by a little green Renault parked outside.

Feeling like Hansel and Gretel, Barney and Lucretia advanced and knocked on the door.

It opened and a face like a little wizened old apple peeped out. Lucretia drew the blanket back from her face a little. "Er – *nous*..." she said. "*Nous* ... er..."

"What does 'noo' mean?" whispered Barney.

"It means 'we'."

"I thought '*oui*' was 'yes'?"

"Shut up! You're putting me off!"

The door opened wider to reveal a neat, clean little old woman with a wrinkled, kindly face and a mop of grey curls. She wore a white apron and held an iron soup ladle.

"*Qu'est-ce qu'il y a?*"

"*Nous sommes* ... er ... *nous sommes ici – voilà!*"

The woman gazed at them uncomprehendingly and let loose a stream of rapid French. Now it was Lucretia's turn to look uncomprehending.

"I thought you said you could speak French?" Barney challenged her.

"I can! She must be speaking a funny dialect."

"We Are Lost," Barney said to the woman, speaking slowly and distinctly. "We Are Camping And We Got Lost." Then, desperate to remove the look of total incomprehension from the old woman's face, he launched into a dumb show: he performed a Scout salute, mimed consulting a map and compass, mimed walking by tramping up and down on the spot, mimed getting lost by turning perplexedly round and round and ended by rubbing his belly and looking plaintive.

The woman stared at them expressionlessly for a long minute and then broke into a smile. She beckoned them in, turned and walked back into the house, leaving the door open behind her. They followed, Barney first politely removing his tea cosy.

They found themselves in a large rustic kitchen, with smoked hams and strings of onions hanging from the rafters and, despite the warmth of the day, a large fire smouldering in the hearth. The old woman shuffled to the stove and heated up for them two bowls of steaming, garlicky soup. They fell on it ravenously while the old woman watched with a benign, unblinking eye.

Edgar's chair lay in ruins amid a tangle of rope now. The front door of the Crow's house was wide open. Huffing and puffing furiously, Edgar pedalled up the road on his bicycle.

Lucretia yawned as she mopped out her bowl with a piece of bread; Barney caught the yawn and sent it back, redoubled. The room was warm, their bellies were full, they had walked all night and it was hard to keep their eyes open.

The old woman released another stream of animated French and motioned them towards the wooden stairs in the corner of the room.

"What shall we do?" said Lucretia. "Can we sleep here?"

"Just a nap, I think," said Barney. "She seems a nice old lady – I'm sure we can trust her."

Outside a squall had sprung up and the raindrops tapped vigorously at the shutters.

They allowed themselves to be ushered up the stairs and shown to a little chamber with a mattress on an iron bedstead. The old woman left them with a grandmotherly smile. Barney put his tea cosy back on and they tumbled into bed.

"We'll have to get up again soon and get on the road before the sun comes back out," cautioned Lucretia. "And before she can alert anyone."

"I don't think she'll alert anyone. Such a nice old

lady. Mind my head!" he added as she snuggled up to him.

"All right, I'm minding it."

Lucretia gave him a little kiss on the lips. That was the last either of them remembered until they were awoken by a frenzied hammering at the door downstairs.

"What— what—?" Barney started and his arms went up instinctively to protect his skull.

"Ssh!"

Lucretia slipped back the bedclothes. She caught Barney's hand and they crept out on to the landing together and peeped down the stairs. There, in the doorway, dripping with rain, stood Edgar, his bulk looming larger by contrast with the little old woman who confronted him. It seemed she never opened the door without a weapon to hand, for she was waving a blazing torch, lit from the fire.

Barney and Lucretia watched, mesmerized, as Edgar went into a confused explanation of his presence in fractured French. Now the old woman seemed to have recognized him; she lowered her torch and began to pay attention. She said something and turned to point up the stairs.

Lucretia came to life. She pulled Barney back out of sight and they ran back into their room. She closed the door noiselessly and turned the key.

"Quick!" she breathed. "The window!"

They tugged it open and, the rain flying in their faces, looked down to the garden below.

"It's not very high," said Lucretia. "And there are bushes to land in."

"But what – ?"

"We're jumping."

"But what about my head?"

"Wrap the blanket around it. Let's go!"

It happened so quickly that Barney had no time to feel scared. He was not acting, simply reacting; it was like watching somebody else clamber over the sill, hang by his hands and drop down into a tangle of bushes, winded but intact.

Lucretia crashed down beside him. They were safe, momentarily. But from above came the sound of splintering wood as Edgar set about putting his shoulder through the bedroom door.

"Quick, let's run for it!"

"No chance. They'd catch us, we wouldn't get fifty metres," whispered Lucretia. "Let's get right in behind this bush – here, next to the wall – and hide that blanket. They might miss us."

Up above, Edgar peered out of the window. "They've skedaddled," he reported. "Not a sign. They've legged it." Then the sound of footsteps retreating.

Lucretia grasped Barney's forearm and squeezed; he understood that she was telling him, don't move, not yet. But it was horribly difficult to remain still as Edgar and the old woman came tramping about the garden searching for them; it was harder by far to do nothing than it had been to jump out of the window.

At one point Edgar moved to within a few feet of them and stared directly at their sheltering bush. Barney felt himself trembling; a raindrop trickled down his neck; he had an itch in his nose, his foot, his bottom; he was going to cough, he was going to sneeze, he was going to cry out . . .

Edgar moved off. "They ain't here," he said. "How long ago did you put them put them up to bed? Three hours? Could be miles away by now."

"*Quoi?*"

"*Je dis* . . . oh, forget it."

The old woman said something.

"Yeah, all right, worth a try, I suppose."

They got into the little green Renault; the windscreen wipers started up; the wheels crunched over the track and they were gone.

"Wow!" said Barney. They emerged stiffly from their hiding-place, scratching their various itches and laughing shakily.

"Now what?"

"Head for the hills," suggested Barney.

"Better get some provisions first."

"But we can't go back in there!"

"Why not? They're looking for us along the road. They won't be back just yet."

Giggling at the audacity of it, they slipped back inside and plundered the kitchen; they stripped it bare, filling two large bags with bread, smoked sausage, cheese, apples and tomatoes, some vegetables they had no means of cooking and some tins they had no means of opening. Lucretia even wanted to take one of the hams hanging from the ceiling, but Barney said it would be too heavy to carry.

Laden with their provisions they emerged and struck out into the uplands. The rain was easing off but the sky was still safely clouded over.

"Lucretia?"

"What?"

"I'd just like to say. . ."

"What?"

"That you were brilliant!"

"Was I?" said Lucretia, pleased. "Yes, I suppose I was. You weren't so bad yourself, Barney-boy."

Edgar and Madame Jabès returned after an hour's fruitless cruising of the neighbouring roads.

"Well, they can't get too far away on foot. But how can we find them?"

"I must call my son."

"Yeah, good idea."

"Victor will know what to do."

"Victor always knows what to do."

"Victor will know what to do without fail."

"Victor's bound to know what to do."

"Victor will know what to do without doubt."

"It's funny," said Edgar, "the Crow thought I was working with Victor. I wasn't – but I am now! Sort of ironic, innit? I tell you what, I'm starving! Have you got any grub in the place?"

Chapter Twelve
A Pain in the Nose

Mickie Trickie had not heard a word from Victor Jabès. He returned to his hotel almost hourly to see whether any message had been left; each time the desk clerk shook his head and smirked as though the idea of anyone's wanting to leave a message for Monsieur Trickie was utterly incredible. Mickie spent the rest of the time wandering around Paris with his eyes peeled in the hope of spotting Jabès or, better still, Barney. He had no luck and his money was getting low. It was time to call Jabès. He set off to find a call-box only two minutes before Annick called his hotel.

Another blank. Annick replaced the receiver, a

clown-like expression of disappointment on her face. The telephone wasn't getting her anywhere. Perhaps she should just get in her car and drive down to Provence, see if Lucretia was all right, find out what, if anything was going on. After all, it was her cottage, wasn't it? At the thought of action her face lit up in a clown-like expression of excitement.

A few minutes later and her little red Citroën 2CV was puttering out of Paris, towards the autoroute that led to Provence.

Mickie Trickie stood in a call-box outside St Lazare station and dialled the number on his Gauloises packet.

"*Allô?*"

"Hello. Monsieur Jabès? Mickie Trickie here."

There was a click and a long silence ensued, so long that Mickie Trickie was on the point of hanging up and trying again, when finally the voice of Victor Jabès sounded in his ear.

"*Allô*, Mr Trickie? Something has come up, my young friend. An emergency has reared its head. Can we meet?"

"Sure."

"Under the clock at Gare du Nord in half an hour – you can manage this?"

"Sure," said Mickie, and hung up.

"OK, what's the low-down?" he said to Jabès when they met. "Shoot."

"Urgent business renders it of the utmost necessity that I depart for Lille immediately. Impossible for me to remain in Paris longer, I fear. I must be on the next train for Lille."

"When will you be back?"

"That, I cannot say. I regret my future plans are now cloaked in uncertainty."

"What about the kid? Any leads on where he's being kept?"

"No, I regret, nothing. At this juncture I can do no more. Something more pressing, you understand..."

"But what am I going to do?" Mickie burst out petulantly.

"Remain here, my friend, and continue your investigations." He threw his thick, powerful arms around Mickie and embraced him Gallicly, kissing him on both cheeks. "*Et bonne chance!*"

"Yeah, sure."

Jabès turned swiftly away. Irresolute, Mickie Trickie watched him go for a moment and then, on an impulse, started to follow. He simply could not allow his only lead to walk out of sight and away from the case.

To Mickie's surprise, Jabès did not go towards any of the platforms nor towards the ticket office. Instead he strode towards the Métro entrance. Keeping a discreet distance behind, Mickie followed him down the steps, purchased a ticket from the machine on the wall and arrived on the platform just in time to get into the carriage next to the one Jabès had boarded. Jabès travelled only one stop. At the next stop, Barbes Rochechouart, he descended and Mickie Trickie descended behind him.

(Here was something else it seemed he had a knack for. Tailing, they called it. Or shadowing.)

They were twenty metres apart as they emerged into the busy Boulevard Rochechouart. Jabès turned briskly into a quiet side-street. Mickie Trickie caught up with him just as he was unlocking the door of a silver Citroën.

"This is the next train to Lille, is it?" Mickie Trickie enquired.

Jabès spun round and a dramatic and terrifying change came over his face. It was like watching Dr Jekyll turn into Mr Hyde, or the transformation of a werewolf at full moon. He lunged at Mickie Trickie and grabbed hold of his nose, twisting it viciously this way and that.

"I offered you a civil and amiable excuse, did I not? Have you not the subtlety, you foolish English booby, to see when you are not wanted? I waste my time, I construct an elegant excuse to leave you with politeness and this is my reward, to be followed by a sneaking boy. Nobody follows Victor Jabès!"

Mickie struggled to break free but the grip was too strong; the terrible twisting went on and on.

"Nobody! If I see you again I will kill you, do you understand? I will cut off your head – I will feed your heart to the pigeons!"

He jumped into his Citroën and sped away, leaving Mickie Trickie leaning against a litter-bin, close to tears.

Victor Jabès put his foot down and the speedometer

needle flickered up to 130 kph as he roared along the autoroute, direction Tarascon. He had received the phone call from his mother that afternoon. Now that Barney was at large, and the Crow's daughter with him, Mickie Trickie had become a redundant figure. They could pick the kids up perfectly well without him; there was no longer any need to send him into the Crow's den.

Jabès always liked to keep his plans as simple as possible. He chuckled in his beard as he thought of the unceremonious way he had disencumbered himself of the boy detective. There would be no more trouble from him.

Dusk was falling as Annick knocked at the door of her cottage. There was no reply and the windows were dark. She turned her key in the lock and went inside. The first thing she saw was one of her favourite chairs scattered in about twenty pieces on the floor as though it had exploded.

Annick looked at it in distress, feeling rather like the little bear in the Goldilocks story. What was going on here? She went back to her car, deciding to drive up to Avignon and see her parents to find out what they thought about it all. Who had smashed up her chair? And where was Lucretia? And why was the boy in the photograph wearing her wolf brooch? And where were the Crow and Stella? The questions lay in a mental heap like a handful of pieces from different jigsaw puzzles.

Chapter Thirteen

An Encounter With Annick

Annick was not to know, of course, that the Crow and Stella were at that moment driving along the very same road as her, just a few kilometres ahead. When they had returned to the cottage to find Edgar gone, the Crow's fury had been such that he had started jumping up and down on the ruins of the chair, demolishing it even further.

"When I get my hands on Edgar, he'll be in a worse state than this chair!" the Crow promised.

"Yes, but where is the toad?"

"He must have gone to where the kids are."

"Yes, but where are they?"

"Jabès has got them, of course!"

"And where's he? They could be on their way to Paris by now!"

"Yes," said the Crow, calming down suddenly. "You're right, Stella. Then we'll go to Paris. We can track Jabès down; I know his haunts. *Nil desperandum*." (Which means "Don't despair" in Latin.)

They jumped into the black limousine and sped off up the road, direction Paris. They were not to know, of course, that Barney and Lucretia were only a few kilometres ahead.

Barney and Lucretia emerged from the copse of trees where they had passed the sunlit hours, brushing twigs from their clothes. It was pleasant to step out into the evening quiet of rural France, a quiet broken only by the chirping of insects. "Cicadas," said Barney knowingly. All around them lay vineyards, brown fields striped with darkening gold vines as far as they could see.

"Er – where are we?" asked Barney.

"I think we're in the middle of some vineyards."

"I can see that! But now what?"

"We must be careful not to get lost."

"*Get* lost?" said Barney. "I think we ought to get back to the road."

"What road?"

"The Avignon road. It must be still down there. Or any road. At least roads go somewhere."

"We might be seen there."

"Yes, and we might be seen here, and shot by a farmer. Come on, let's go."

Leaving behind the tins they couldn't open and the vegetables they couldn't cook, they threaded their way down through the terraced slopes and came eventually to the road they had left earlier that morning, or one very like it. Barney was feeling pleased with himself. If only Jeremy Carver could see him now, he would find nothing to make fun of. Since Lucretia had elected him her kidnapper he seemed to be growing more resourceful, more decisive; more hero material. As if to prove it another inspiration struck him.

"Why don't we hitchhike?"

"Because it's dangerous."

"Dangerous? I'm starting to forget what that word means."

"It means risky," Lucretia told him patiently. "Harmful to the health."

"But we've got to take risks now. We're in a risky situation. The next car that comes . . ."

The next car was coming and at the sight of it they both leapt into the ditch. Barney landed full-length and only just managed to save his skull from contact with the ground. Lucretia helped him to his feet.

"That was my dad!"

"I know." Barney had recognized the car; it was the same black limousine that had whisked him away from St Cuthbert's.

"They're out looking for us!"

"No kidding," said Barney, glad of the chance to be sarcastic at Lucretia's expense for once. But though he spoke bravely he was shaken. That fleeting glimpse of the Crow and his wife in their ominous funereal car had brought back to him the nightmare of captivity.

"I told you it was risky," Lucretia reminded him.

They clambered back on to the road and Barney defiantly stuck out his thumb.

"At least we know they've gone now."

"Yes, but Edgar and that nasty old lady are still

looking for us. Maybe the next car along . . ."

But the next car along was a little red Citroën 2CV driven by a young woman. It came puttering along towards them and stopped.

"*Où allez-vous?*"

"Avignon. Paris. Calais."

The woman smiled at them and opened the door. She had a pleasant, friendly face which, with its wide mouth and mop of curly blonde hair, put one in mind of a circus clown. They got in, Lucretia taking the front seat. She stared curiously at the woman. It was eight years since she had last seen Annick and her mental picture of her had become very blurred. No click of recognition came; yet the woman's face seemed strangely familiar.

"What's your name?" she asked.

"Anne," replied Annick. She had learned that English people usually got her name wrong and decided she might as well save them the trouble.

"Oh," said Lucretia.

Annick looked at her curiously. Lucretia had naturally changed a lot in the last eight years; besides, her usually pale face was streaked with mud where she had dived into the ditch, so it was hardly surprising that Annick didn't recognize her. Nevertheless, the child's face seemed strangely familiar ...

"And what is your name?" she asked.

"My name? ... It's Sophie," said Lucretia. It wouldn't do to give her true name, on the run as she was.

"Ah," said Annick, feeling obscurely disappointed. She cast a quick glance over her shoulder at the boy sitting in the back. The boy's face, too, was daubed with mud, and he wore a most peculiar hat – some sort of a cushion, it looked like – which came down to his eyebrows. As it happened his wolf brooch lay hidden in shadow, and Annick did not connect him with the boy she had seen in the photograph.

"And your name ...?" she said.

"Oh, it's ... wait a minute ..." said Barney. He mustn't give his real name, being not only on the run but a kidnapper into the bargain, but every name in the world except his own had gone out of his head. "My name, yes, well, it's ..."

"Go on, tell her your name, Richard," said Lucretia, trying to be helpful. But just at that moment inspiration had come to Barney.

"Peter," he said.

"But what is it," queried Annick, "Peter or Richard?"

"Oh, well, it's both. I've got two names. Richard Peter – I mean Peter Richard," said Barney, deciding that sounded better.

Annick laughed and didn't pursue the question. She and Lucretia were soon getting on well, chattering erratically about the scenery in French as they bowled along; but presently Lucretia's supply of French gave out and they switched back to English.

"What are two such young peoples doing alone on the road? And in a strange land?"

"Oh, we're in the Scouts," said Lucretia, taking up the story that Barney had mimed to the old woman and improving it. "We're doing our Foreign Hiking badge."

"The Scouts?" said Annick – except that she pronounced it "Scoots" – looking sidelong at Lucretia.

"Well, it's sort of like Scouts and Guides mixed. It's a mixed troop, very modern. We're called the Young Adventurers."

"But you 'ave no uniforms?"

"Oh, we don't believe in uniforms in the Young Adventurers. Nasty things!"

"Why, nasty?"

"Old-fashioned, I mean. Too soldier-ish. So we were on this Foreign Hiking trip – sort of long-range orienteering – to get our Long-Range Orienteering badge."

"Badges, then, are not old-fashioned?"

"No, badges are OK. They're a very modern design, they're holographs, in fact." Barney, listening in the back seat, could only marvel at her powers of invention. "And then we got lost, you see," Lucretia went on. "Stranded. And we've got to meet the rest of the troop in Calais tomorrow."

"But for orienteering you 'ave a map, no?"

"Yes, we had a map but a gust of wind blew it away. And we dropped our compass in a pond. Well, *he* did."

"No, I didn't!" protested Barney.

"Yes, you did. And he dropped our packed lunch in a bog," she confided to Annick.

"You 'ave no luck!" said Annick, laughing. She opened the glove compartment and took out a bunch of bananas. "If you are 'ungry, with the lunch in the bog, you may eat these."

"Ooh, thanks!"

"And 'itch-'iking, that is allowed in the Young Adventurers? 'Itch-'iking can be dangerous for young peoples."

"Oh yes, but we're encouraged to use our initiative in the Young Adventurers. We'll probably get an extra badge for it, in fact. An Initiative badge."

"With a 'olograph!" said Annick, and laughed again.

Gradually, they were leaving the countryside behind them. Houses, shops and garages began to appear at the roadside, sparsely at first and then in greater profusion.

"Soon we are in Avignon," said Annick. "I stop 'ere tonight. But tomorrow I go on to Paris. I can take you there – if you like to stay with me tonight."

Lucretia cast a look back at Barney. As they had already discovered, it was difficult to tell whether you could trust somebody when you didn't speak the same language. But this woman seemed trustworthy if anyone did. Barney gave a nod.

"Ooh, yes, please," said Lucretia. "If it's no trouble."

"*Mais non.*"

She pointed out for them some of the sights of old Avignon as they passed through: here was the famous bridge in the famous song, only half of it standing now; there the palace where a rival Pope had once ruled; here a park with a red English telephone box in it, a gift from the people of Colchester. Suddenly she turned into a narrow, twisty street and parked, as the French will, at an angle of forty-five degrees to the kerb.

"I 'ave a call to make – could you wait one moment?"

She disappeared up the steps of a large public building. The building stood out from the others in the dark street because a French flag hung over the door and the porch was illuminated by two electric lanterns; on each lantern was written the word "Police".

Barney and Lucretia looked at each other. Then, without a word, they were out of the car and pelting down the street.

At the bottom they almost ran into a bus about to

pull away from the stop. The doors opened, they climbed on. Lucretia tendered a ten-franc piece.

"*Deux, s'il-vous-plaît.*"

"*Beau chapeau, monsieur,*" said the driver to Barney.

"What did he say?" asked Barney as they sat down.

"He said you're wearing a nice hat."

They giggled about this for the rest of the journey. The journey ended when they reached the outskirts of town. They jumped off and started walking.

"I'm sure this is taking us back the way we came," said Barney.

"Yes, but we can't go back through town now. We'll have to skirt round it. The police will be looking for us."

"Why can't we let them find us, then?"

"You're a kidnapper now. You'd get sent to prison."

"Don't be stupid! They'd know it was only a joke. The quickest way for us to get home would be to go to the police. We shouldn't have run away back there."

"Yes, we should. I told you I can't shop my mum

and dad to the cops – and you promised no police,"
Lucretia reminded him. "Come on, we need
another lift, quickly. You're conspicuous with that
tea cosy on your head."

They stuck out their thumbs.

A silver Citroën screeched to a halt and a large,
bearded man leaned out of the window.

"Jump in, children," said Victor Jabès.

Something about his face warned them to run for
it. But they hadn't got more than a few paces before
he caught them up and seized them each by an arm.
He pushed them into the back of the car.

The door slammed.

And they were off.

Victor Jabès was laughing so hard they could
barely hear themselves scream.

Chapter Fourteen

Mr Spofforth Gets a Fright

Mickie Trickie was thinking hard. Desperately hard. His only lead had vanished. He had tried phoning the number on his Gauloises packet again but each time he got through somebody hung up on him. He had returned to the café where he had met Jabès but had encountered only blankness, hostility and derision. The option of going to the police occurred to him but he rejected it. He wanted personal revenge on Jabès. His nose was still painful whenever he blew it or sneezed, and this happened often, because Jabès's assault seemed to have brought a cold on.

He sat on a green park bench in the Jardin des Tuileries with his detective's hat tipped low over his eyes and thought hard. Desperately hard. Suppose he did go to the police, what could he tell them? He could furnish a pretty detailed description of Jabès: age mid-forties, weight sixteen stone (what was that in kilos?), build broad and thickset, dark hair, full beard, round little nose, chunky gold ring, etc., etc. So far so good. He could describe the man's car and give the registration number, he had a contact telephone number or an ex-contact one, he knew the bar where he had met him. This was all excellent material for the police but it was slender stuff for Mickie Trickie, operating alone, to work on.

Was there nothing else? Nothing at all? He squeezed his memory, squeezed it hard as though trying to extract the last drop of juice from a dry lemon.

There was the postcard Jabès had been writing...

The postcard. "*Chère Maman*," it began. "Dear Mum", that meant. And the address? The address! What was it? He brought the scene back into his mind: he could see the postcard clearly enough, there on the marble-topped table with Jabès's stubby fingers pushing the pen across it ... but the words of the address refused to come clear.

But the address must be there, somewhere in his memory banks. He had seen it; and Mickie believed that everything he had ever seen was stowed away in some recess of his brain. There was no doubt about its being in there; the trouble was getting it out again.

He tried a technique he had often used successfully in calling up buried observations: that of flexing the mind, like a muscle, straining to remember, then letting it relax and grow limp ... then flexing again ... then relaxing ... until ...

Until finally, during one of his relaxed moments, the answer floated gently to the surface.

Madame Jabès, Rue des Lapins, Tarascon, Provence.

A short time later Mickie Trickie was sitting comfortably aboard a TGV (*Train à Grande Vitesse*, or Very Fast Train) bound for Tarascon. He settled down behind the copy of *Le Monde* he had bought at the station kiosk; he couldn't read it, but it seemed fitting to carry a French newspaper on a French train. He felt calm and ready for action now that he was on his way; the hours spent waiting for the train had been tense. He had filled in the time by eating a frankfurter coated with mustard and inserted into a crusty French baguette – not the same as the hot dogs American detectives like Marlowe fed on, but probably much nicer – and by telephoning Mr Spofforth to tell him about the latest development in the case. Spofforth was out at his factory, overseeing the installation of a new parsnip-masher, but Mickie had left a message with his wife.

The TGV glided speedily and silently through the dark suburbs and out into the darker countryside. He wouldn't arrive at Tarascon until well into the evening but that suited his plans. A detective banging on your door after nightfall was calculated to scare anyone into spilling the beans.

"Did you have a good day at the factory, dear?" asked Mrs Spofforth sweetly as her husband hung up his hat in the hall.

"Yes. The new machine is really first-rate."

"And the new taster? How's he settling in?"

"Oh, him? Yes, he's first-rate, too. A first-rate chap."

"He's a good worker, is he?"

"Certainly. He's been tasting away like a good 'un."

"That's funny," said Mrs Spofforth. "He called me from France today."

Mr Spofforth opened his mouth, but nothing came out.

"How would you explain that?"

Mr Spofforth rallied. "I – I sent him there to taste some soup. French onion. Er ... we're thinking of using the recipe here, under licence, that's it."

"I see. And what did he mean when he said the case was going well?"

"Ah – obviously, he meant the case of soup we ordered for him to taste."

The next moment Mr Spofforth felt as if he were on the receiving end of a hurricane. His usually docile wife was transformed into a stormy, raving madwoman. And it frightened him. He backed against the wall as she advanced. She was shouting into his face, hurtful things, violent things and – worst of all – true things.

"That boy wasn't a soup-taster at all, was he? He was a detective! You're trying to get out of paying the ransom, aren't you? You grubby old miser!"

Her hands grasped his shirt-front.

"Please, be reasonable, my dear..."

"How dare you call me dear! I'm not your dear – you don't like dear things, do you? You like cheap things, things that save you money!"

"I'm sorry you feel that way, but—"

"You'll be sorry all right if Barney's been damaged. I'll drown you in a vat of your own soup! I'll mash you up in your own parsnip-masher!"

"I'm sure that won't be necessary..."

"You've heard from the kidnappers, haven't you?" said Mrs Spofforth suddenly. "I know you have. You've had a letter and you didn't tell me. Where is it?"

"I – I received a small note – I didn't want to bother you..."

"Where is it?"

"Possibly – er – a small message might be found – in the drawer of my desk..."

Mrs Spofforth pounced on the drawer and pulled out the letter. She opened it. A lock of Barney's hair fell out.

Mrs Spofforth gave her husband a look that nearly knocked him over.

"We're going to see Inspector Belcher. Now."

"Do you think—"

"Put your hat on!"

As they drove to the police station Mr Spofforth seemed to have aged ten years. He hunched over the steering-wheel, his shoulders sagged, his whole face drooped. He looked so guilty and woebegone that Mrs Spofforth almost – but not quite – felt a twinge of sympathy for him.

Chapter Fifteen

A Mexican Stand-Off

The silver Citroën sped smoothly along, gobbling up the kilometres between it and Tarascon.

"So sorry you could not stay longer last time," said Victor Jabès. "My mother was not expecting you. Now we shall be able to extend some real hospitality of the region. You can stay with us for a good long time."

"You'd better let us go," said Lucretia defiantly, "or my dad will come and sort you out."

"No, no," said Jabès, laughing jovially. "If Monsieur Corbeau pokes his beak in, it is I who will sort *him* out. You have it the wrong way round!"

Lucretia let out a sudden cry.

"Why do you squeak?" enquired Victor Jabès.

"None of your business," Lucretia told him. She did not think it politic to explain that she had just seen her mother and father pass by in their black limousine.

"Did you see what I just saw?" asked the Crow.

"Yes! Stop the car!"

The Crow slammed on the brakes and performed a snarling U-turn.

They pursued the silver Citroën at a safe distance, keeping it just in sight. The Crow's hands gripped the steering-wheel like the talons of a hawk clutching its prey.

"Beep beep!" sang Victor Jabès as he honked the horn. Madame Jabès, followed by Edgar, appeared at the door. Their eyes widened in delighted surprise when they saw who was in the back of the car.

"You've got them!"

"Oh yes. Trust Victor."

Madame Jabès beamed on her son, like a proud mother whose son is taking curtain calls after performing the lead role in the school play.

"Into the house with them!"

Surrounded by their grinning captors the children were taken inside. Madame Jabès and her son were gabbling vivaciously in French; Edgar executed a shuffling, comical dance, waggling his bottom as he went over to the kitchen range to make some coffee. A party atmosphere reigned. Barney edged closer to Lucretia and they squeezed hands.

"But look!" shouted Victor. "The two young persons are holding hands! Is not young love delightful? For it makes the world turn round, no matter what dry old scientists may say!"

At that moment there came the sound of a car pulling up just outside. Everybody froze and stared at each other.

The door crashed open and there stood the wild, vampiric figure of the Crow. His face was alive with triumph and anger; the gaunt, vengeful face of Stella peered over his shoulder.

The Crow reached into the pocket of his long black coat, took out his small gilt box and munched on a liquorice spider.

Still nobody moved.

Then Stella lunged forward, grabbed hold of

Barney, who was nearest the door, and clutched him to her. "Got you!"

"I came, I saw, I conquered," pronounced the Crow. "As Julius Caesar said."

But he had wasted time by his words. As he moved to take back his daughter, Madame Jabès seized her and bundled her over to the fireplace. She snatched out a burning brand and held it over Lucretia's head. She shrieked something in French.

"She says she'll set light to the girl's hair if you take one step closer," translated Victor Jabès. "Well done, Mother. Checkmate, I think, Monsieur Corbeau? Edgar, go and get the boy."

Without leaving hold of Barney, Stella snatched up the iron soup ladle from the kitchen table. She plucked Barney's tea cosy off and held the ladle above his head.

"You come one step closer, Edgar, and I'll crack his skull like an egg."

"Careful. The boy's worth money," Barney heard the bearded man say.

"Not with his brains all over the floor he isn't."

It was a Mexican stand-off. Barney ran through the position in his mind, surprising himself by his

175

coolness. Both he and Lucretia were in danger and both were worth money. But the chances of his coming to grief seemed slightly greater. Lucretia was worth money only to Victor Jabès – and it was Victor Jabès who held her. If he, Barney, got his skull cracked, then Jabès would still have a bargaining counter. On the other hand, they couldn't expect to get as much money for Lucretia as for him, since her parents were not as rich as his. Jabès's hope must be to get the greater prize by trading Lucretia for him. But then the Crow would be left with nothing, except his daughter back, and though he naturally wished her to come to no harm he must be holding out for some return on his investment, hoping to bluff Jabès into giving Lucretia up.

"The sword of Damocles is hanging over the boy's head," said the Crow. "It won't hang there for ever. Stella's arm is getting tired." Barney felt a tickling sensation in his scalp at these words. "We want our daughter back. You'd better decide."

Victor laughed. "There is nothing to decide. We have your daughter. Give us the boy if you want her back."

Of course it would not help the Crow to have

Barney killed because then his bargaining counter would be gone. But in a tense situation like this, could he be counted on to act logically?

Victor and the Crow had stopped arguing and were staring hard into each other's eyes. The tension was unbearable. Who would make the first move, Barney wondered – or would nobody make it, would they all remain standing here like dummies in a tableau until they fainted from hunger and exhaustion? He put his hand in his pocket to fondle his comforting little wooden duck. But it wasn't there. Of course – Lucretia had it. His hand went to his lapel and he stroked Lucretia's silver wolf brooch instead.

The farmhouse clock on the wall ticked noisily. The brand over Lucretia's head crackled and spat. A foot above his own head Barney could feel, though not see, the iron ladle hovering.

Chapter Sixteen
The Great Escape

Mickie Trickie made his way along the dark country road with stealthy, gliding steps. A quiet excitement possessed him. He was walking into danger, perhaps; but they didn't know he was coming, whereas he, obviously, did. This gave him the sense of being at an advantage.

"I'm on the case," he said to himself. "Trickie's on the case."

Ahead, he saw the lights of a cottage. It looked friendly and cheerful. He unfolded the map he had bought at the station and shone his torch on it. This was the place, all right. As he put the map back in his pocket a red Citroën 2CV drew up beside him and a young woman poked her head out.

Mickie Trickie turned his torch on her, making her blink. This time she wasn't wearing a light-blue jumper but a lime-green one. But she had the same blonde frizzy hair and the same broad, clown-like face. Mickie cocked his thumb and pointed his index finger at her as though aiming a gun.

"Annick," he said.

"Ah! But we met in Paris!"

"Right. We meet again."

"You are Trickie Dickie."

"No, I'm not. I'm Mickie Trickie," said Mickie Trickie, slightly annoyed.

"*Mais comme c'est bizarre, et comme c'est curieux, et quelle coincidence!*"

"If you say so."

"I stop because . . . 'ave you seen two childrens on the road?"

"Two? No. I'm looking for one."

"For one? Ah, you mean the boy in the photo?"

Mickie Trickie bit his lip. He was the detective; it should be him asking the questions.

"Who are you looking for?" he asked abruptly.

"I saw two childrens today. They were lost. The boy wore a strange 'at. I take them to the police station but they run away. I become worried. I drive along the road to search them.''

"Uh-huh," said Mickie Trickie noncommittally. The boy wore a strange hat? Then it could be Barney, seeking to protect his head. But the other child?

"What about the other kid? What did they look like?"

"A girl. Muddy face. Dark 'air.''

"I see," said Mickie Trickie, not seeing. But this woman seemed trustworthy. She was on the level. He wondered whether to enlist her as an ally. A potentially dangerous situation lay ahead – he might well be outnumbered and an ally could be valuable. His mind made itself up.

"I'll be straight with you, madame," he said. "I'm a private detective and I'm looking for the boy. The one with the strange hat. He's been kidnapped. And I've every reason to suspect that the inhabitant of that cottage can tell me something about it. The boy might even be being held there – maybe the girl too.''

"That cottage down there?"

"That very one. I'm on my way to rescue the boy.

Right now. If you'd care to lend a hand..."

"What will you do?"

"First I'm going to make a recce – a reconnaissance, that is," he added as Annick looked puzzled. "I'm going to creep down there. Softly softly. See what I can see. Interested?"

"Yes, I will come," said Annick simply.

"You're a cool customer, Annick," said Mickie. "Got to hand it to you. Now we've got to be dead quiet. Kill the motor. We'll advance on foot."

"OK."

"Let's go!"

They crept down the lane cautiously, tiptoed through the gate. Shielded by the night they advanced right up to the yellow rectangle of the window. The shutters were open and they were able to see right into the room.

It was like standing in front of a picture in a gallery; like a picture, too, in the stillness of the figures there. The Crow, Stella and Barney were grouped by the door; on the other side of the kitchen table, nearer the window, stood Madame Jabès, Edgar, Lucretia and the man Mickie recognized as Victor Jabès. He noted the upraised ladle, the threatening brand of fire.

He tugged Annick's sleeve and they retreated to the gate.

"Looks like a tricky situation," said Mickie Trickie. "Two gangs in there."

"I know one gang!" said Annick. "It is Stella and her Crow man. And the girl – but it must be little Lucretia!"

"The boy's Barney, that's for sure," said Mickie Trickie. "And I know the man with the beard. It's Victor Jabès, a very dangerous character. We'll have to watch out for our noses."

"What will we do?"

"Catch them by surprise. Bluff them. You've got a phone in your car, haven't you? Phone up and ask to speak to Madame Jabès. Tell her the house is surrounded."

"But the number?"

"90 91 90 13."

"How do you know?"

"It's written on the telephone on the table," said Mickie Trickie. "I notice these things. It's my job."

"And then?"

"Don't hang up. Don't say goodbye. Run back

here and bust in through the door. I'm taking the window. Ready?"

"Ready."

"Let's go."

Mickie stationed himself by the window and waited. He forced himself to take slow, deep breaths. He knew the phone was going to ring and they didn't. The thought calmed him.

He saw the Crow take a little box out of his pocket and eat what appeared to be a live spider.

"That doesn't frighten anyone, Dad," came Lucretia's voice. "They're only made of liquorice."

"*Liquorice?*" said Edgar.

The telephone went off. Mickie saw the occupants of the room start nervously and felt a thrill of satisfaction.

"Get that, Edgar," he heard Victor Jabès say.

Edgar picked up the receiver.

"'*Allô?* It's for you," he said, holding out the phone to Madame Jabès.

"Can't you see she's busy, you fool?" barked Victor.

The moment had come. Mickie Trickie took hold

of the two sides of the window and threw them apart.

"I suppose you're wondering why I've called this meeting," he said pleasantly, leaning into the room.

After that things happened rather quickly. Victor turned and saw Mickie Trickie. "You!" he hissed. He rushed towards the window.

Mickie Trickie stepped back and brought the shutters crashing together on Jabès's body, knocking the wind out of him. Jabès lay across the sill, half in and half out of the room, struggling for breath. Mickie seized his beard and gave it a furious twist.

"That's for my nose," he said, "and that –" here he gave the beard an even more savage twist – "is also for my nose!"

He opened the windows again and let Jabès slump back to the floor. Mickie Trickie put his leg over the sill and climbed into the room.

"Don't anybody move," he said. "The house is surrounded."

Edgar, who had still been trying to explain in his tortured French that Madame Jabès was otherwise engaged, let the phone drop with a clatter.

The Crow was the first to recover his wits.

"No, don't *you* move," he told Mickie Trickie. "We've still got the boy."

Stella waved the ladle menacingly. At that moment the door behind her burst open, Annick plucked the ladle from her hand and dealt her a stunning blow over the head with it. She tottered and collapsed.

The Crow moved to wrest the ladle from Annick – when Edgar suddenly came to life.

"Liquorice!" he shouted. "They were only made of liquorice. You made me eat spiders and you didn't even eat them yourself!"

He hurled himself at the Crow and knocked him to the ground. He knelt astride his chest and proceeded to batter with his fists the cruel tyrant who had force-fed him spiders.

Mickie Trickie and Annick advanced slowly on Madame Jabès.

"Come on, let the kid go," said Mickie Trickie. "It's all up with you."

Madame Jabès unleashed a torrent of vicious-sounding French, the purport of which was clearly that she would set Lucretia's hair aflame at the next step forward.

And it was then that Barney made his move.

Completely regardless of the risk to his skull he plunged forward and cannoned into Madame Jabès, knocking her arm with his elbow so that the burning torch flew from her hand and went arching across the room to land on the seat of Edgar's trousers. Edgar leaped up with a howl. The Crow, who had had quite enough, remained on the floor. Madame Jabès aimed a blow at Barney's head, missed and reeled backwards.

Mickie Trickie grabbed Barney's hand; Annick grabbed Lucretia's; a moment later and they were out of the door, sprinting up the lane to Annick's car.

They piled in, the key turned in the ignition and they were away.

"Er – who are you?" said Barney.

"I'm the detective who's rescued you," said Mickie Trickie proudly.

"And I know who you are," said Lucretia to Annick, suddenly. "You're my auntie Annick!"

She burst out laughing. And the next minute the car was filled with laughter as they all joined in.

Then their laughter died away as a pair of headlights appeared in the distance behind them.

The villains had recovered, declared a temporary alliance and were giving chase. Annick stepped on the accelerator but the silver Citroën DS was much faster than her little 2CV. The headlights were getting bigger.

"They're gaining," said Mickie Trickie.

Annick picked up the car phone and called the police.

"You know the number by heart?" said Mickie Trickie, impressed.

"Of course. The Chief of Police in Avignon, you see..."

"Is your father," finished Mickie Trickie.

"My mother, in fact."

Two squad cars came racing past them, sirens blaring.

Mickie Trickie sank back in his seat, put his hands behind his head and stretched out his legs. What would his auntie Meg have to say about this? He had solved his first case.

Chapter Seventeen
Barney Back at School

"**H**ey, Barrrney!"

"It's Barrrney!"

"He's come back from Frrrance," said Jeremy Carver. "He's rrrreturned from Frrrrance!"

Barney stood in the Remove Common Room once again, wearing his St Cuthbert's uniform, the fluorescent strip lighting glinting off his plastic helmet.

"Yes, I'm back," he said.

Gregory Snood produced a copy of a newspaper and pointed at a photograph on the front page. After the escape, and after the Crows and the Jabèses and Edgar had been taken to prison to await trial, Barney and Lucretia had been escorted to Paris by

Mickie Trickie and Annick, where they were met by Barney's parents, Inspector Belcher and a crowd of press photographers.

"This is you, isn't it?" said Gregory.

"Well, it looks like me," said Barney. "And it's got my name underneath. So you must be very intelligent if you've worked out that it *is* me."

There was a wave of laughter at this unexpected sally and Gregory Snood blinked his eyes in surprise. Barney smiled, pleased with himself. After what he had been through he was finding the St Cuthbert's boys nothing to get alarmed about. And the time he had spent with Lucretia had sharpened up his bantering skills considerably.

Jeremy Carver entered the fray. "This old guy's your dad the soup-maker, isn't he?" he said, indicating the picture again. Barney acknowledged that it was. "Doesn't look too pleased to see you, does he?"

It had to be said that he did not. When they had met in Paris, Barney's mother had returned to Barney his lock of hair, pressing it into his hand, and Barney had not forgotten the shamed, beseeching, hoping-to-be-forgiven look his father had worn as she did so. Since then Barney's father was a changed man. He seemed humbler, older, gentler. When they had got home he had taken Barney aside and told him in mumbling tones how sorry he was and that he loved Barney dearly and did Barney realize that? Barney had felt so sorry for him that he forgave him on the spot.

Barney's mother was even more changed. The balance of power in the Spofforth household had shifted decisively in her favour. She was learning to drive and had started French lessons. And with the growth in her confidence she was less protective towards Barney. She thought of him as one who had been through the kiln of adventure and got hardened.

"Doesn't look too happy at all," went on Jeremy. "Wasn't he glad to see you back?"

"He was glad to see my face, not my back," said Barney.

This raised an even bigger wave of laughter.

"Oh," said Jeremy Carver sarcastically, "you discovered *wit* while you were abroad, did you?"

"Well, I wouldn't be likely to discover it *here*, would I?" returned Barney.

It was game, set and match.

"Barney Spofforth?" The long neck and mild, round head of Mr Pargeter came poking through the doorway. "There's a parcel for you here. From France."

Barney took the parcel and examined it.

"Who's that from, Spoffo?"

"I think it's from Lucretia. She's a girl I was with in France. She's in the photograph, look."

"Ooh, yes. She's pretty, isn't she?"

"Pretty ugly, if you ask me," Jeremy Carver chipped in, but this time no one bothered to laugh.

"Yes, she's a lovely girl," said Barney casually. "She helped me escape."

"Tell us all about it."

"Later, later," Barney promised. "Let me open my parcel."

He tore off the paper. Inside was another package and a note, dated "Some time or other".

The note read: "*Dear* Barney, I hope you're as well as I am!! I'm living with Annick now – it's *lovely*!!! And I go to the lycée and my French is getting *brilliant*!!! We've moved north to Lille, lots of nice cloudy skies for me to play under, nasty old sun hardly shows his face! I think of you *lots* – what an

exciting time we had!!! I'd *really* like to see you again
– Annick says you can come and stay at Christmas,
would you like that? Write to me *soon*!! I'm
enclosing a little present for you – wear it with *pride*!!
Lots of love, LUCRETIA."

"What does it say, Spoffo?"

Barney folded the note and put it in his pocket. "I
think that's between me and Lucretia," he said
coolly. "And now let's see what's in this package."

He tore it open and took out a French beret,
padded on the inside with steel plates sewn into it.
He took off his plastic bonnet; the beret clinked
slightly as he fitted it over his scalp. He twisted it just
a little askew as he smiled jauntily at the crowd of
admirers surrounding him.